THEORIES OF EVERYTHING

PRAISE FOR THEORIES OF
EVERYTHING

"These fifteen stories vary widely in terms of subject matter, theme, setting, and characters, yet they are unified by the strength of the writing and the narrative voice . . . there is an energy in all of these stories that propels and seduces the reader and piques her interest. And what a variety of characters! Academics, street people, ageing hippies, farmers, music producers, videogame players and their mothers, movie stars, boxers, actors, cooks, and even a parrot. The writer clearly has compassion and affection for the characters he's created and put through their paces, sometimes with laugh-out-loud humour."

— J. JILL ROBINSON, AUTHOR OF *THE LAND OF NOT KNOWING*

THEORIES OF EVERYTHING

DWAYNE BRENNA

THEORIES OF EVERYTHING
By Dwayne Brenna

Shadowpaw Press
Regina, Saskatchewan, Canada
www.shadowpawpress.com

Edited by Dave Margoshes

Cover created by Bibliofic Designs
Yin/Yang symbol by Dan Carter

Trade Paperback ISBN: 978-1-998273-29-4
Ebook ISBN: 978-1-998273-30-0

Shadowpaw Press is grateful for
the financial support of Creative Saskatchewan.

CONTENTS

Savage God	1
Los Diablitos	14
Resurrection	24
Respite	34
Meeting Tiffany Sloane	45
Isla Mujeres	60
Collateral Damage	73
How To Be Happy	88
Crop Circles	102
War Wonton	114
Big Oil	124
The Sewing Machine	136
Train Ride with Busconi	149
Blood-Red Polish	158
Theory of Everything	166
Acknowledgments	181
About Dwayne Brenna	183
About Shadowpaw Press	185
Available or Coming Soon	186

For my sons

SAVAGE GOD

THERE THEY ARE, these two aged hippies, skin the colour of seashells bleached by salt and sun. One of them is pushing a wheelchair, leaning his skinny frame on it so he won't fall over. The other guy is in the wheelchair, three spliffs short of a brain cell, drooling and mumbling out directions. They could be twins. They're longhairs with tinder ponytails, identical black leather trousers and vests, both of them wearing those sunglasses that look like welder's goggles, the leather casings clawed in tight around their eyes. Good thing it's nearly dusk, or they might spontaneously combust.

Rick and I are coming out of a seafood place near the Inner Harbour. We're in town to watch a couple of hip-hop acts, same old same old. Rick turns to me and says, "You know who that is, don't you?"

"Should I?"

"Yeah, you should," he says. "That's Ramsay Baudelaire."

"The guy in the wheelchair?"

Rick looks at me like I'm a fool. "The one who's still upright," he says, very droll.

I'm old enough to have listened to Baudelaire in the '60s. He wore whiteface and devil's makeup, three inches thick, for all his concerts and album covers. You never saw a photo of him unless he was wearing makeup. "How do you know?" I ask.

"It's common knowledge in these parts," Rick tells me. He's clearly delighted that his knowledge of ancient rock surpasses mine. "He lives just around the corner at the Juan de Fuca."

"*The* Ramsay Baudelaire? As in, Ramsay Baudelaire and the Flowers of Evil?"

"The one and only," he says. "Not up to much anymore, though."

The two codgers stop on the sidewalk nearby, but I don't think they notice us. Ramsay produces a white handkerchief from his leather trousers and blows the nose of the guy in the wheelchair. I get a closer look at the two of them. Ramsay's got fingers about a foot long; no wonder he was the best axeman of his era. The face of the guy in the wheelchair is deformed, and his growl is surly, Alzheimerish. It's clear that Ramsay likes the guy, though, or he wouldn't be digging loogies out of the drooler's nose.

Ramsay grins, and his teeth are as yellow as an old horse's. "Do you know who I am?" he asks his buddy in the wheelchair.

The drooling guy's face contorts into a mask of anger. "Your name," the man growls, "is Fucked If I Know."

Ramsay stuffs the snotty handkerchief into his pocket and wheels his buddy down to the walk light. When the light changes, he edges the wheelchair gently over the curb, and the two men disappear around a corner.

"Who's the guy in the wheelchair?" I ask.

"That's a conundrum," Rick replies. "Some say he's Ramsay's brother. Some say he's an old bandmate. Some say they used to be lovers. No one knows for sure."

"Man," I tell him, "I used to listen to those guys every night when I was twelve years old. My forty-five of 'Cynara' got so scratched and dented from over-use that the only way I could enjoy it was to melt it down and sniff the acetone."

SOMEHOW, the image of those two aging rockers sticks with me for the next month and a half. I can't shake it. I'm intrigued by the enigma of it and also by the romance. The way Ramsay wheeled his buddy around made me think that the promises of the 1960s had been kept. Hippies were still hippies and not the businessmen that most of them later became, and rockers like Ramsay were still brothers-in-arms like they said they would always be.

The image haunts me, especially where I work.

On a cold November day, when I've got little else to do, I find myself at the computer, Googling Ramsay Baudelaire. "Internationally famous rock guitarist, born in Vancouver, Canada, in 1947," *Wikipedia* tells me, "best known for his debut album, *The Sacred and the Profane*." I read, to my surprise, that Ramsay's real name is Robert E. Cummins and that he had a pronounced stutter as a child. I already knew that he'd suffered a stroke in Paris when he was in his mid-forties, after a binge of heavy drinking and drug use, and that his band, The Flowers of Evil, broke up shortly after that. *Wikipedia* doesn't say much about his life from that point on. There's a grainy photograph of Ramsay in concert at the top of the page. It sure doesn't look much like the Ramsay I saw at the Inner Harbour, but what did I expect? Bob Dylan doesn't look much like Bob Dylan anymore.

I talk to Rick about the possibility of bringing Ramsay into the studio. He says I'm out of touch. "You saw the guy, Ken," Rick says to me. "He's one log short of a log roll."

"He didn't look so bad," I say. "Those old rockers might forget their own address, but they never forget how to play."

Rick accuses me of wanting to reclaim my lost youth. "I'm not gonna pay for your delusions," he tells me. "You can rent the studio from me if you're that obsessed with the guy."

EARLY ONE MORNING IN DECEMBER, I dial the number for the front desk at the Juan de Fuca Inn and speak to the desk clerk there. "Can you put me through to Ramsay Baudelaire's room, please?"

The desk clerk has a nasal twang that could loosen your fillings. "I'm afraid, sir, that nobody by that name is registered at this hotel."

I have to think fast. What did *Wikipedia* say his name was? "Robert," I blurt into the phone, and then I remember the rest of it. "Robert Cummins. Is he staying there?"

"Oh, Bob," she twangs. "He's in one of our suites. I'll put you through."

I hear the sounds of somebody fumbling with a telephone, and then I'm patched through to Ramsay's phone. It rings about a hundred times. Finally, as if he's been playing a waiting game and tired of it, Ramsay picks up. "What?" he says in a voice that's far away, maybe somewhere back in Mariposa. He sounds a little like Dylan and a little like a space cadet. If marijuana could talk, it would have a voice like Ramsay Baudelaire's.

I pause for a second. What do I call him? Bob or Ramsay? I decide that it's more respectful to address him by his stage name. I know how rock stars feel about that sort of thing. "Is this Ramsay?" There's another pause a beluga could swim through as Ramsay summons up the wherewithal to answer. Has he been toking this early in the morning? Of course, he has. "Am I speaking to Mister Ramsay Baudelaire?" I ask quickly, in case he decides to hang up.

"Yeah, man, that's what they call me," he says, sounding curiously sunny.

"I just wanted to introduce myself," I say. "My name is Ken Graham. I'm a sound engineer at AMI studios in Vancouver." My mouth is motoring along like Maybelline at the top of the hill.

"Is this, like, one of those syndicated robocalls?" Ramsay asks. "Because, like, man, I gave at the office if you know what I mean." He's a little slow on the uptake, and his conversation is littered with "likes" and "mans," but no sign of a stutter so far. I expected a stutter, even just a slight vestige of the one that tainted his childhood, and I'm a little disappointed when I don't hear one. Maybe he overcame it in his high school years. Or maybe the stroke reconfigured his brain, and his stutter was gone.

"This isn't a telemarketing call!" I'm almost shouting into the phone. "I just want—I just want to set up a meeting with you."

He processes this. "Who the fuck is this, really?"

"I work at a studio in Vancouver," I blurt into the phone. "I wanted to talk about recording some of your songs. I'd be happy to take the ferry across. We could meet right there at the Juan de Fuca. In the pub or somewhere."

"I'm always up for a beer," he says. "So is Everett."

"Maybe next Saturday?" I say. "I could take the late ferry. Be there by two in the afternoon."

There's no response. I hear him breathe into the phone for about a minute, and then he hangs up.

THE JUAN DE Fuca Inn is a neat little affair on a back street behind Beacon Hill Park. It's less costly than most of the hotels two blocks down at the Inner Harbour, and it attracts fewer tourists. Like many hotels in Victoria, its interior attempts to revive some Canadian notion of what Britain used to be, all oak walls and brass ceilings.

I'm sitting at one of the tables in the attached pub at quarter to two, nursing a cup of coffee. At three, I go to the front desk and dial Ramsay's room. The phone rings interminably, and then Ramsay picks up.

"Mister Baudelaire," I say into the phone. "It's Ken Graham."

"Who?"

"We were supposed to meet in the pub downstairs an hour ago."

"Shithouse mouse," he says hoarsely. "We'll be there in a heartbeat, man."

At three-thirty, Ramsay strolls in, rocking the same leather trousers and vest he had on last summer. His head is covered with a bandana, the way bikers wear bandanas before they put on their helmets, and he's still accessorizing with his welder's goggles. He's pushing his buddy, who is also decked out in leathers and a bandana and welder's goggles, in the wheelchair. I wave from my table, and they approach.

"Mister Baudelaire," I say. "It's good to meet you finally."

"Yeah, man, likewise," he says, offering me an unsteady high-five. He jerks a thumb at the guy in the wheelchair. "This is my buddy, Everett. He goes with me everywhere."

"Pleased to meet you, Everett," I say. Everett looks away.

"Everett doesn't talk to strangers," Ramsay says. "I do his talking for him."

After the beer arrives and everyone's comfortable, I open up the conversation. "Do you still play?"

"You mean the guitar?" Ramsay drawls with a sidelong look at his companion. "Yeah, man, I play every day. Use it or lose it, man. Know what I mean?" He takes a nervous drink.

Everett, meanwhile, chugs his beer, and it dribbles down his chin.

"I think I mentioned that I'm a sound engineer over at AMI," I tell him. "I'd like you to come in and cut a demo of 'Cynara.'"

"A demo?" Ramsay asks as if he's not quite sure what a demo is.

"Yeah," I say. "A re-recording of the song. Only this time with all the bells and whistles that the twenty-first century can afford."

He looks down into his beer glass for the reply that is percolating in the yellow frothy soup. "Dunno," he growls, looking like the hull of an ancient ship that's just been recovered from the bottom of Florencia Bay.

I jump in again. "I didn't mean to scare you," I say. "The bells and whistles are your choice. You'll have complete artistic control. But it'll be a tidier recording than anything you could have produced in—when was it?—1968?"

He glances at Everett, and Everett stares off into the distance as though the men's washroom sign is of vital importance to him. "It's been a long time," Ramsay says. "And I don't have a band anymore."

"I'll bring in the best session players in Vancouver," I assure him, taking a sip of my coffee and trying to be nonchalant. "What's the worst that could happen? We fall on our faces, and the demo never sees the light of day."

"I'll give it some thought," he says.

I realize now that I'm coming on way too strong with the demo idea, and I decide to backtrack. "I'm your biggest fan," I tell him. "I lost my virginity in the back seat of a Galaxy 500 as 'The Orphan's New Year's Gifts' played on the eight-track."

Ramsay snickers into his beer glass. "Goddamn eight-tracks had good sound quality."

"My girlfriend thought so."

"Glad we could be of assistance." He shoots Everett an alcoholic leer. "Aren't we, Everett?"

"Piss off," Everett says, looking down at the soiled hardwood.

It's amazing how much these two guys look alike, even though one side of Everett's face is slumped and immobile. I guess people start to look like one another after they've lived together for a long time. "Is it true that you once nailed a Playboy Bunny in an elevator in Chicago?" I ask.

"I can't remember, man," Ramsay says. "That would be wrong on so many levels, wouldn't it?" He wheezes and chortles at his own joke and drinks some beer to punctuate it. Everett looks stone-faced at the washroom door.

Ramsay seems to enjoy talking about the past, even the parts he doesn't remember, so I tilt the conversation in that direction. He glories in his salmon fishing expedition with Jethro Tull, remembering that Jethro was a great musician but a better fisherman. He tells a story about accidentally shooting his own drummer in the leg with an illegal handgun in a hotel room in Santa Monica. Charges were pressed but later dropped, he says. He vaguely remembers a party in Andy Warhol's apartment. "That fucking Scottish-soup-can connoisseur," Ramsay calls him.

Everett turns to him and shouts, "Asshole!" at the top of his lungs. The entire pub is looking at us. Everett quaffs the rest of his beer and slams his glass down on the table with a thud. Even Ramsay realizes that this is a bit much, and we talk in whispers for a while.

All the stories Ramsay tells are public knowledge—some of them even appeared on *Wikipedia*—but Ramsay loves telling them, so I listen. We talk into the early evening, until the waitress brings me the bill. "It was such a pleasure meeting you," I say to Ramsay. "Please promise that you'll consider recording with me at AMI." I hand him my card. "You can call me at this number."

He peers at the card through his welder's goggles. "Ken Graham?" he reads like he's never heard my name before. "You a businessman, Ken?"

"Just a sound engineer," I tell him, "and a fan of your music."

TWO YEARS PASS. I've been busy in the meantime, recording all these hip-hop guys, some black, some white, all of them trying to cash in on millennial angst. On the way to work one day, I'm listening to a Golden Oldies station. "Here's a blast from the past," the deejay intones, "Ramsay Baudelaire and the Flowers of Evil." He plays 'The Orphan's New Year's Gifts.' If I were thirty years younger, I'd have to stop and masturbate.

I find myself phoning Ramsay, later that morning. "Hey Ramsay," I say. "It's Ken Graham. Remember me?"

There's a longer pause than I expected. "You an insurance salesman?"

"I'm the dude who met with you a couple of years back," I say. "About coming in and recording a demo."

"Just a sec." He puts the phone down and goes somewhere. When he picks up the receiver again, a couple of minutes later, he says, "Name a time."

My heart starts pounding. "We could record sometime next month," I tell him. "What day of the week works for you?"

"Any day," he says.

"How about Monday the fifth?"

"Groovy."

"I'll come and pick you up myself," I tell him. "We'll take the ferry across."

THE FERRY RIDE from Victoria to Vancouver is a little choppy because of the rain, but that doesn't stop Ramsay from going out on the deck and hanging over the rail. "I'm King of the World," he shouts, mimicking Leonardo DiCaprio in *Titanic.*

Everett and I are sitting sensibly inside as the ferry bunny-hops over the waves. Everett is looking off into the distance. Ramsay's famous Stratocaster is reclining in a hard grey case at Everett's feet.

Ramsay enjoys it all a little too much. He careens across the deck like a drunken sailor as the rain pelts down on him. When he comes back inside, his grey hair is awash, and the rain has beaded on his leather duds. "The Georgia Strait," he drawls. "Fucking awesome."

Later, on the way to the studio, he marvels at the logging barges heading up the Fraser River, at the height of the high-rises in the downtown core. "Nothin' like that in good old Victoria," he says. He's like a kid in Disneyland for the first time.

When we're out of the car, and I'm unloading Everett's wheelchair from the trunk, Ramsay retrieves his guitar case and stands at the entrance of the studio. The rain is pelting down on him, but he's impervious. He's almost vibrating with excitement.

In the foyer, I introduce Ramsay to the receptionist and to Rick. Ramsay's not as interested in people, though, as he is in the two fish that inhabit the aquarium behind the receptionist's desk. "The clownfish protects the anemone from predators," I tell Ramsay since he's so interested, "and the anemone provides a home for the clownfish."

"Kinda like me and Everett," he drawls.

"Oh yeah?"

"Not sure if I'm the clownfish or the anemone, though."

I've hired a bunch of the best studio musicians in the city to play with Ramsay. Jordan, the drummer, comes in looking like he was sitting in a jazz club till three in the morning. He probably was. "I'm really looking forward to this," Jordan says, shaking Ramsay's hand. "I've heard a lot about you."

Ramsay offers up a riddle. "What do you call a guy who can't read music but hangs around with musicians?"

"A roadie?" I reply.

"No," he says, "a drummer."

Jordan looks down at the floor. Ramsay blathers on and on, and I begin to wonder how high he is. Higher even than he was on the boat.

Luckily my bass player, Kevin, appears in the doorway at that moment. I introduce him to Ramsay. "I listened to your record last night," Kevin says. "You're a fucking genius." Kevin's all of twenty-three.

"Yeah, well," Ramsay replies, "call me when you're a fucking genius, too."

Kevin just grins.

Ramsay insists that Everett sits in on the session, not just in the control room but in the studio. I have my misgivings about the idea, but I relent because Ramsay seems so tied to the old codger. When we're in the studio, Ramsay fumbles with the clasps on his guitar case. He holds the axe gingerly in his bony hands, licks his lips, and strums. The Strat is badly out of tune. Finally, Ramsay hands the guitar to Kevin. "Think you can tune this?"

Kevin shrugs and tunes the guitar.

"Okay," I say when Ramsay's got the guitar in his hands again. "We'll have a few practice runs, and then we'll lay down a track."

"These guys know the song?" Ramsay asks.

"They've had the music for a couple of weeks," I tell him.

Ramsay saunters over to Everett and places the tuned guitar squarely into his lap. Everett wants nothing to do with it. He drops the guitar on the carpeted floor with a reverberating clang. "Fuck off," he mutters.

"You promised," Ramsay pleads. "You promised you would if I made it happen."

"Stupid fuckin' roadie," Everett hisses. "I ain't gonna play."

The session players are looking at me dumbfounded, and I'm

trying to make sense of what I see before me. "What's going on?" I ask.

"You want the real Ramsay Baudelaire?" the guy who's been calling himself Ramsay says. "He's sitting right in front of you."

I look at Everett. He growls at me like an old dog.

"He's suffered in silence all these years," the fake Ramsay says. "It's time he claimed his rightful place. And this was the only way I could make it happen."

I hesitate, and then I point at Everett. "Do you mean . . .?"

There's a guitar intro for "Cynara" that rips your heart out. The first time I heard it, back in 1968, I thought of angels and waterfalls. I heard it with my spine and with my perineum, not with my ears. I've waited two years to hear Ramsay Baudelaire play it again in my studio, but it turns out he's a stroke victim in a wheelchair.

"It's the arthritis," the fake Ramsay says. "Makes his hands numb, and he thinks he can't play no more." I don't bother telling the guy that it's cost me twenty-five hundred of my own money to rent the studio and the session players.

Jordan and Kevin take fifteen while the artist formerly known as Ramsay and I adjourn to the control booth for a refreshment. I pour him a coffee mug full of vodka, and he slurps it down like a derelict on Granville Street. He's shaken. "Sorry all to hell about this," he says. "I did it for Ramsay, ya know."

"Hey, no worries," I tell him. "Have your drink and relax."

"He was a great guitar man," the guy says, taking another gulp of vodka.

I look at him squarely. "He was the greatest guitar man of his generation," I tell him, and I mean it. "Better than Harrison. Better than Santana." Tears are welling in the guy's eyes. "What's your name?" I ask him, just out of interest.

"Doesn't matter," he says with a sheepish look on his sallow face. "I ain't nothing but a lowly roadie, just like Everett says."

Someone must have left the mikes open in the studio because, at that moment, I hear the opening bars of 'Cynara,' so mournful and yet so full of hope that I wonder if I'm imagining it. It's a rusty rendition of the old tune but unmistakable. The sure-handedness is still there, the lack of a slide as the frets are ascended. My youth comes back to me, and I'm in the back seat of that Galaxy 500 again with Emily Sidlowski. I hear angels and waterfalls.

When I peer through the window into the darkened studio, I see Everett sitting in his wheelchair behind a mike stand with the Stratocaster in his hands. His fingers are meaty now, but he bends the steel strings deftly. His eyes are closed, his head tilted heavenward, and he looks like a pale white savage communing with the gods.

When his mouth opens, the words spew out like a torrent of lava. The devil himself could not sing it better or with more ferocity.

LOS DIABLITOS

STANDING in the doorway of her ancient house, Dona Esmeralda watches the celebration. She doesn't like what the fiesta has become. It was once a celebration of her people's indomitable spirit. They had never given in to the Spanish *conquistadores*. Her forefathers and mothers had lurked in the Borucan jungle like *los diablitos*, little devils, waiting for the opportune moment. They had painted their faces with the geometry of warfare.

Nowadays, the fiesta has become a drunken affair, an excuse to roam from house to house, demanding alcohol. The sacrificial bull, representative of the Spanish and their bullish ways, is all but forgotten. An old woman now and one of the few who speak the language of her ancestors, she knows that even the masks have changed; the little devils are painted sometimes to represent the anti-Christ, not the bringers of chaos that used to inhabit these Telemanca mountains.

Esmeralda watches in disgust as the men don their costumes so they can perform the rituals of *los diablitos* out of season. A tourist bus has arrived, having traversed the Highway of Doom from San Jose. The *gringos* have come to Costa Rica to see a fiesta, and a fiesta is what they will see. When, she wonders, will the real *diablitos* return? She stares down at the stains of purple dye on her hands, on her shirt and her torn blue jeans. Perhaps the women will have to show the way.

IT IS SPRING NOW. She likes the *gringo* the first time he appears in the village. There is something affable and generous about the man, standing there in his khakis and his broad-brimmed hat. He's arrived in a beaten-up Land Rover covered with dust. He stands at Esmeralda's door and says *hola*. That is the full extent of his Spanish; he relies on his driver for an introduction.

"This is Senor Jerry Hyman," the driver says. "He is the owner of the Puntarenas Eco Village Resort. He would very much like to make your acquaintance."

Esmeralda holds out her hand, and the *gringo* shakes it. All *gringos* are tall, but this man is even taller than most. He towers over Esmeralda like a mountain. "Nice to meet you," he says in English. Esmeralda nods her head and smiles.

Apparently, Dona Esmeralda needs no introduction. The driver does not even bother to say her name and the *gringo* seems to know who she is. She wonders what he thinks of her, an old lady now, with glasses purchased from a travelling optometrist, her hair tied back severely. Does he think she will be a pushover?

They walk up the road to the craft pavilion together, the *gringo* talking incessantly about the mountains and the river. "Isn't it bad," he says through his translator, "that the government is damming the Terrabas? Will it affect the water supply to the village?"

Inside the pavilion, the masks are laid out on white sheets that cover the hand-hewn, rough wooden tables. Some of the masks have been painted, others have not. They range in price from fifteen thousand to forty-five thousand *colones*. Imagine, Esmeralda thinks, the temerity of old Carlos to demand forty-five thousand *colones* for his work. No one will ever buy at such an exorbitant price.

There are also woven tapestries hanging from the walls at Esmeralda's insistence. Why should the men be paid for their work and not the women? Carving masks is painstaking work, but is it not also painstaking to collect the dyes for the tapestry? Is it not painstaking work to sit and weave for days on end? Still, the tapestries are not worth as much as the masks; they sell for ten thousand *colones* each.

Esmeralda explains about the masks and the tapestries. "The masks are made of balsa that grows here. The painted masks are for the tourists. The unpainted ones will be used in the fiesta and then burned."

"They are very beautiful," she hears the *gringo* say.

"The colours in the tapestries all have meaning," she continues. "The purple is our royal colour. The dye is milked from snails that live on the coastline near your resort."

The driver and the *gringo* exchange words in English, and then the driver turns to Esmeralda. "He will take them all."

Esmeralda is taken aback. "All? The masks or the tapestries?"

"Everything," the driver says.

Esmeralda looks at the *gringo*. "Does he want a special price?" she asks.

"He wants to be a friend of your people," the driver replies. "He will pay full price and sell your wares at his boutique."

A little piqued at not having had the opportunity to barter, Dona Esmeralda responds with a taut "very well." She turns the masks over, one by one, and begins to calculate the total price. Then, she adds the cost of the tapestries. Her heart is pounding as she hands the gringo a piece of paper on which the sum is written.

Three hundred and seventy thousand *colones*. The biggest sale she's ever seen. Esmeralda feels a little like a devil lurking in the jungle as the *conquistadores* pass by. She wonders if the man knows how badly he has negotiated for the masks.

The *gringo* opens his wallet and pays her the full amount.

YOUNG RODRIGO MORALES drives the old truck, the radio blaring his beloved rock and roll. Dona Esmeralda rides in the cab with her granddaughter, Sanchita. Other women of the village are jostled mercilessly in the box of the truck as they trammel westward along the bumpy roads. It is time to go in search of the colour purple.

The road through the mountains is a treacherous one, but Rodrigo goes slow. They meet truckloads of Panamanian workers on the way, migrants looking to help with the pineapple harvest in the north. Occasionally, there is a police car on the side of the road, and Dona Esmeralda grows tense. The police have not proven friendly to the Borucan people. Best to leave them alone.

When they arrive at the coastal highway, Esmeralda rejoices in the pocked asphalt on the road; her old bones will survive the remainder of the journey. Along the highway are many resorts owned by Americans. Each of them is fronted by a stern metal gate, sometimes with signs on them that say "Keep Out." Dona Esmeralda understands what "Keep Out" means. Men patrol the gates. These are the traditional hunting grounds of Dona Esmeralda's people, and yet they have been forbidden access to the coastline as each new resort is built.

The *gringo* from Puntarenas, Senor Jerry Hyman, the one who bought the masks, is their hope now. Dona Esmeralda had seen fairness in the man's eyes when he came to the village. Some of the other women were skeptical, never having met the man, but Esmeralda assured them that he was not like the other *gringos.*

She is surprised, though, by the closed metal gate that stands at the entrance to the Eco Village. A guard, who has been sitting in the gatehouse, comes out to meet them. He eyes the brightly dressed women in the truck box derisively, then proceeds to the driver's side window. "What is your business here?" he asks in Spanish.

"We are here for the snails," young Rodrigo replies.

"Snails," says the guard with an abrupt laugh. "There are no snails here."

"There have always been snails here," Dona Esmeralda interjects. "This is where our people have come for many generations to milk the snails."

The guard looks at her, his mouth set. "There is nothing here for you now."

Before he can walk away, Dona Esmeralda says, "We would like to speak with Senor Hyman."

The guard's eyes are full of rage at this bit of name-dropping. "Senor Hyman?" he says curtly. "Do you know Senor Hyman?"

"He visited our village two weeks ago," Esmeralda says. "He bought our masks."

"Senor Hyman is a very busy man," the guard says.

"You should call him nevertheless," says Esmeralda. "He would be disappointed if he found out we were here and could not see him."

The guard stares at Esmeralda, appraising her resolve. At last, he says, "Very well. I will call." He goes into the gatehouse and stays there for a long time.

When he returns, he is particularly jocund. "Senor Hyman cannot see you," he says, smiling broadly at Esmeralda. "He is out of the country, on business."

"When will he return?" Esmeralda asks.

"Who knows?" the guard replies. "Maybe a week. Maybe a month."

SEVERAL OF THE women are in the craft pavilion, spinning brown cotton into thread. Because she is the eldest, Dona Esmeralda supervises the making of the dyes. The greens and blues are easy, made from boiling leaves in large vats. Black is messy and has to be saved for late in the process when bark from the *carbonero* tree is boiled down. Purple is the saddest colour now. It is made from a small cask of manufactured dye found in a shop in San Jose and sent by bus to the reserve.

Some of the women card wool, others sit at the spinning wheel. Dona Esmeralda's arms are discoloured to the elbow with greens and blacks and purples. There is still joy in the process, however, with the women gathered together as they have always gathered. They work, and they laugh, and they tell stories about each other and about the men who have been part of their lives. "Did you hear what Carlos did with his ill-gotten gains?" one woman asks. "He went into town and bought some floor polish."

"He can spend his money as he pleases," says another woman.

"Yes," continues the first woman, "but Carlos lives in a shack with a dirt floor!"

The women are still laughing when the rusty Land Rover comes chugging down the dirt road to the village. The vehicle creaks to a stop near the craft pavilion, and the driver and the *gringo* get out. The two men confer for a moment, and then they approach the women.

"*Hola*," says the driver.

"*Hola*," says Dona Esmeralda, hardly looking up from her vat of dye.

"Senor Jerry Hyman would like to buy your wares," the driver says.

"Our wares are not for sale to Senor Jerry Hyman," Esmeralda responds.

The other women stop working for a moment, looking from Esmeralda to the driver to the *gringo* standing behind him. They know about the lucrative sale of the masks a month earlier, and they do not want to miss out on such a sale again. "But Dona Esmeralda—" one of them begins to say.

"Our wares are not for sale," Esmeralda repeats firmly.

The driver speaks to the *gringo* in English, and the *gringo* speaks back.

"He says to tell you that he is a friend of your people," the driver announces to the assembled women. "He wants only what is best for you. He has sold all of your masks to the tourists. Now, he would like to buy your weaving at the price you ask."

The women exchange glances. One of them, the second eldest in the group, frowns at Esmeralda, but Esmeralda silences her with a stern look.

"Our product is flawed this year," Esmeralda continues. "We have had to use store-bought dye."

"That will make no difference to the tourists," the driver answers quickly. "They cannot tell the store-bought dye from the rest."

"Yes, but we can tell," Esmeralda says, "and that makes our product substandard."

Again the driver and the *gringo* confer.

"He will pay five hundred thousand *colones* for all your tapestry," the driver says to the women.

Some of the women gasp at the mention of such a grand sum. Dona Esmeralda looks at the driver coolly. "Why did your man turn us away when we came to collect our dye?"

The driver is impatient now. Esmeralda can hear it in his

voice, even as he speaks again to the *gringo*. The *gringo* takes off his hat and wipes the sweat from his forehead. He speaks to the driver in anxious tones, all the while looking at Esmeralda. "Senor Jerry Hyman says that he would be happy to receive Dona Esmeralda at his resort," the driver says to Esmeralda, "but he is concerned that the tourists get very worried when there are many people that they do not know in the resort."

"These are our traditional hunting lands," says Esmeralda.

"There is also a question of security," continues the driver. "What if one of your people steals the wallet of one of our guests? What then?"

"My people are not thieves," Esmeralda says plainly. "My people are good people."

"That is a chance Senor Jerry Hyman cannot take."

Esmeralda scowls at the driver. "Then we have nothing more to say."

"Are you sure?" the driver asks. His voice is rising. "Are you sure that you want to put an end to our arrangement?"

The other women stare at Esmeralda for a long time.

"I am sure," she says quietly.

THE BORUCAN WOMEN return to Senor Hyman's resort the next spring. They set off in young Rodrigo Morales' truck in the early evening before the sun has begun to disappear behind the Telemancas. The women sing songs of their past as they bounce along the narrow roads, but they stop singing when they turn onto the coastal highway. Rodrigo even turns off his beloved radio. It is a ghost truck he drives, purring down the highway as the sun disappears and the fingernail of the first quarter moon hangs like an ancient boat over the ocean. Quietly, Dona Esmeralda explains the tides to her granddaughter. "The tides are lowest," she says, "at the first quarter and last quarter of the moon. The snails are exposed, but there will not be much light by which to see."

Rodrigo slows down as they near the sign for the Eco Village. The gate is shrouded in darkness, and there is no evidence that a guard is attending it. Perhaps he is in the gatehouse, sleeping.

They proceed past the gate and down the road until they find another approach in which to park, this one gated like the others but with no sign. When Rodrigo kills the engine, the women disembark. "We must be very quiet," Esmeralda warns them. "One word might betray us."

"Do you know the way from here?" one of the women asks Esmeralda.

"I think I do," she says. "It will take us over uneven ground."

Young Rodrigo stays with the truck to keep a lookout. The women, young and old, follow Dona Esmeralda into the jungle. They walk in single file through rocky terrain. In the dark, low-hanging branches claw at their clothing. Tall grass whips at their legs. The mosquitoes are bad, but the monkeys and the toucans have gone to sleep. Esmeralda's guides are the moon when she can see it and the ceaseless lapping of seawater on the shore.

Half an hour later, they come to a clearing above the shore-line. Esmeralda can hear voices from the Eco Village off to the north, maybe three hundred metres away. There is the sound of music, as well, Mexican marimbas or something like that. She puts her finger to her lips to quiet the women behind her, and then she gets down on her hands and knees and crawls through the tall grass to the edge of the rocky escarpment. The rest of the women follow in like fashion.

Once they are below the escarpment, they are out of sight of the tourists and they can again stand up. They walk in silence to the rocky beach. The women who are in jeans, like Esmeralda, roll up their pant legs, kick off their shoes and wade into the water among the rocks. In the faint light of the first quarter of the moon, they can see the grey shells of the precious snails clinging to the boulders.

Gently, Esmeralda coaxes the shell of the snail from the rock and shows it to her granddaughter. The snail wriggles in her hand. Softly, she casts her breath over the mucous gland of the snail. It secretes a milky liquid into a glass jar that Sanchita holds. In the jar, as if by magic, the liquid turns yellow and then green and then blue and then the royal Tyrian purple. Even in the moonlight, Sanchita can see the colours change.

"You can milk the snail twice," Esmeralda says to her grand-daughter, "or even three times. But no more than that. After the third time, the snail is exhausted, and it needs to rest. Or it will die."

Other women clamour over the rocks, finding snails and taking their precious milk. Esmeralda looks up at the moon and smiles. *The little devils have returned*, she thinks. *They have taken back their ancient lands. They are with us now.*

RESURRECTION

"LIFE IS NOT A VIDEOGAME," my mom said to me last night. It was three in the morning, actually, and I was lying in bed with the controller in my hands. Trying to set up a garrison in PVE mode.

It's a little more like a videogame than she thinks, though, a kill-or-be-killed world out there. She's been trying to set up a garrison of her own for the last three years, ever since she lost her job at Walmart and had to take the night shift at Mister Sub. She always said it was me and her against the world ever since my dad phoned down from Fort MacMurray to say that he wouldn't be coming home no more. What we needed was a spirit healer to resurrect us and set us free.

Some people don't believe in resurrections, but my mom does. She's always going on about the Bible and resurrections and Lazarus and "up from the grave he arose."

"I worry about you, Trevor," my mom said in that moaning voice of hers. She sat down on the edge of my bed. "You're not sleeping good again."

"I get enough sleep."

Her eyes were red and round. "What time are you going in to work tomorrow?"

"Couple of hours from now." I wasn't looking at her, only glancing over every once in a while. At Level 60, you can't take your eyes off the screen for too long at a time. I fire-casted and incinerated a whole army of humans.

"You need to get your sleep," she whined. "It isn't healthy."

"It's good practice for what I do."

"Are you still having trouble at work?" She's referring to my partner Sherman and what she calls his tendency to bully.

"Nah," I say, "it's all good." I got a plan to put Sherman in his place, once and for all.

My mom's kind of skinny, so it's easy to forget that she's there, even when she's sitting on your bed. Skinniness has its advantages, though. She can sneak in and out of rooms like a Wisp. "They're closing down the Mister Sub," she said.

I said, "What?" I mean, are there going to be no more Mister Subs in Canada?

She nodded her head slowly. She always sounds like she's about ready to cry. "Making room for another strip mall," she said, kind of sad but kind of angry too. "And Christmas coming on."

My mom used to wait for Santa Claus to show up. Now she's waiting for rigor mortis. She always loved Christmas, though, and she was always making decorations for down at the church. And she always bought me something nice. Last year, it was a PS3 game console that she bought from the used gaming store, even though she said it was against her better judgment because she thinks I'm too much of a loner. She made me go to the Christmas Eve service in the church before I got to use it, though.

I didn't want to make too big a deal out of the Mister Sub closing because I knew how sad my mom was, so I just kept incinerating humans. If my Australian buddy TechnoGeek59 could have seen me, he would have said how totally rad I was.

"They gave me a month's notice," my mom said, with her voice deep in her throat. "At least we can pay the December rent. I don't know about January, though."

"Don't worry," I said. "Something good's going to happen."

"I wish I could be sure of that," she said. "I was thinking, if you could chip in a little bit with part of your salary . . .?"

I paused the game and tossed the controller down on my ratty old quilt. "You said if I took this job, I could keep whatever I made!" I don't know why I freaked out about it. All the money I make goes into keeping my Kia Rio on the road. Maybe I was upset because Ivor Stormchild was mounting an offensive against me or maybe it was because I was tired like she said.

"You could really help out," my mom whined. "Until I get my feet back on the ground."

"Let's talk about it tomorrow," I said. I wanted her to get out of my room. Go and bring somebody else down for a while and come back when I'm not versing anybody on the PS3. She put her hand on my arm for a second, and then she got up and picked her way through the piles of dirty clothes that were lying on the floor.

This town is no good for me, and I'm no good for it. That's why they kicked me out of college a couple of years ago. They said I was a danger to myself and to the other students because I had violent tendencies. I had violent tendencies because that's the way of the world. It's dog-eat-dog out there. Luckily for me, the college doesn't give its expulsion reports to the police unless you've committed a chargeable offence.

WHEN I FIRST STARTED DRIVING FOR the security company, I thought it was going to be the perfect fit for me.

Because I like a life of adventure and I know how to get out of tough places.

All the company wanted was a valid driver's licence, a high school diploma, and eligibility for carrying weapons, and I had all of that, with no previous convictions because I don't smoke dope. The company has its own day school where they tell you about situations that might arise. They gave me some driving lessons, and they showed me how to shoot a Smith and Wesson M&P. And then they put me behind the wheel.

The driver's never supposed to get out of the truck unless there's an emergency or you're back in the compound. I didn't like that rule very much. Any good gamer knows that you got to anticipate. You can't stand there flatfooted and wait for the emergency to come to you.

I drive with this guy, Sherman. He is the Messenger and also the ATM Technician, which I guess puts him in a different realm than me. The Messenger is just the fancy name they give to the guy who rides in the back, the one who goes in and opens up the ATM or whatever. Sherman used to be in the army, in Bosnia or somewhere.

At first, I thought he was pretty cool, but then I noticed that he freaked out whenever there was a loud noise. Like one time, he was getting out of the truck, and this motorcycle went by, probably a Harley since it had that throaty sound coming out of the muffler. Sherman almost pissed himself. He crouched down beside the truck like a scared puppy, and he waited for the sound to go away. I'm pretty sure that old Herbert, down at the office, wouldn't have been too happy with that. Somebody must have messed up on the background check.

Sherman calls me Bruce Willis. He calls me that because I like to pull my gun out when we get back to the compound. Even though there's razor wire all around it, you never know if there might be someone hiding behind the other trucks. You can't be too careful, that's what Herbert says. But Sherman calls me Bruce Willis, I guess because I look like I want to shoot something. And I do want to shoot something. I just want to squeeze the trigger at something other than a gun range target for a change. I'd like to kill a robber and be given a medal for heroism from the Mayor or somebody. "Hey, Bruce Willis," Sherman says. "It's okay. We're back inside the compound. There ain't no bad guys in here."

Sherman is wrong, though. You can't be too careful. There's bad guys everywhere, lurking in the darkest places. Sometimes, they're standing right in front of you.

See, Sherman thinks he's better than me because he fought in the army and all. What he doesn't know is that, while he was over there in Bosnia getting PTSD, I was quietly up in my room saving Korangar from the human invaders.

I heard Sherman talking to Herbert about me once, just a couple of months after I was hired. It was summertime, and I'd come in from the truck to get a drink of water. When I heard what they were saying, I went into ghost mode, pasting myself against the wall outside Herbert's office. "He's a little spacey," I heard Sherman say. "Like, sometimes he's hyper-alert and looking for action and other times he's a brother from another planet."

"Any evidence of drug use?" Herbert asked him. Herbert's got a voice like Archmage Khaladkar from the video game, and it carries. You half expect to hear some soundtrack music like "Skadi Returns" or something. He's kind of like the mage who sends me and Sherman out on quests, or maybe he's more than that. Maybe he's the guy who invented the game.

"Never saw him using," Sherman replied in a low whisper, "but I wouldn't put it past him."

That's when I knew Sherman wasn't exactly my best friend. Up until then, I thought we were brothers-in-arms, kind of a guild, storming the bastions of the Northern Lands together. Sometimes, it pays to get a drink of water.

After that, things got kind of tense between me and Sherman. Like in the coffee room, he was always putting me down for something in front of the other drivers. "You shoulda seen Willis in action today," he told everybody, one time after a run to the mall. "Some teenager in a leather jacket accidentally bumped into me when I was coming through the door, and Willis was out of the truck with his revolver drawn shouting, 'Everybody freeze!' "

They all laughed.

"Everybody freeze?" Sherman pressed his finger into my chest. "That's old school, Willis." It didn't seem to bother Sherman that he could have gotten me into a shitload of trouble by saying that. Drivers aren't supposed to get out of the truck. And I only did it because I was trying to cover his ass.

I can't say I didn't think about shooting Sherman right there in the coffee room. Putting him out of his soldier-ass misery.

COUPLE OF MONTHS LATER, it was my turn to go to the boss about him. "Herbert," I said. "I'm worried about Sherman."

"Oh?" Herbert was sitting behind his desk, finishing up some paperwork. He looked at me over his glasses.

"He's getting weird," I said. "It's like every time he hears a loud noise, he goes ballistic."

Herbert took off his glasses and rubbed his eyes. He looked at me for a long time, and it was like looking into the eyes of one of the Old Gods. "Sherman's been with us for fifteen years," he said. "I know he's got his problems, and he has those problems because he served his country with honour."

"I'm just saying he could be a liability."

"You've been with us for six months," Herbert went on. "Which one of you do you think is the more expendable?"

There wasn't much more to say after that.

SO, this morning, when I got to work at six o'clock like they want me to, Herbert wasn't there. He'd tacked our itinerary on the bulletin board outside the coffee room. Itinerary, he calls it, but I like to think of it as a quest chain. We go to all these banks and ATMs and whatever, and we pick up useful things along the way. Not like golden rings or breastplates or fire-casting techniques but money that can be used to buy good stuff. Like an AK47 assault rifle or a new Corvette that looks like the Batmobile. And I always learn something while I'm out there questing, just like any good MMORPG should make you do. This job is easy to learn but hard to master.

I always start by Googling the best routes on my phone, the routes that don't take you past any known danger points like parks with grassy knolls or high buildings where snipers could be hiding. Then I clean my pistol, a nine-millimetre double action. That baby can put down a Panderita at thirty paces.

"Whatcha cleanin' that gun for?" Sherman laughed. He was standing outside the coffee room, looking in. I didn't see him until he spoke. "You're never gonna use it, Willis." There was a cup of Tim's in his hand. He didn't bring one for me.

"Who knows?" I said. "Maybe I'll use it today."

Sherman smiled that shit-eating smile of his. "Well, you just keep livin' in your fantasy world, Willis."

If I had to peg Sherman as a character in a video game, I'd say he used to be a Tank, all gung-ho and ready to shoot. He could have been a Healer if he wanted to be, but Sherman doesn't know nothing about healing.

Me, I'm more like a mage, although I play several characters when I'm gaming. I'm best as a mage, though, storing my fire-power until the time is right. I'm pretty focused. It's like I get this one idea in my mind, and I never let go of it.

I had one idea in my head this morning. *I'm a born killer.*

"We better get rollin', Willis," Sherman said. "I gotta be at my kid's Christmas concert at two o'clock."

Once we were in the truck, it was as if I had bought some new superpower that made me see the world in colour while everyone else saw it in black and white. Buildings seemed to jump right off their foundations at me. I passed people walking on the sidewalks, and I could read their thoughts. I could probably pick out of a lineup anybody I saw walking on those sidewalks.

My headphones got all staticky for a minute, and then I heard Sherman say, "Hey, Willis, you drove by that bank twice already."

"Just checking the place out," I said into the microphone.

Sherman laughed, but it wasn't a happy laugh. "Well, stop fuckin' checkin' the place out," he said, "and let me go inside and get the money."

We had nine stops on the itinerary, including five banks, so I knew there would be a shitload of cash in the back when we went back to the compound. I also knew it would be floating around back there loose because Sherman doesn't like to play by the rules. See, the rules say the Messenger's supposed to put the cash in the drop box, anything over a thousand dollars, and the drop box is opened with a microchip that's back at the compound. That's what the rules say. But Sherman doesn't play by the rules. He likes to ride in the back with a satchel of cash between his feet. Says it makes him feel like he's riding shotgun on a stagecoach in the Wild West. Sometimes, there's a half a million dollars in that satchel.

All the while, he's yapping at me over the headset, all low-level bullshit like how I should stop pulling my pud up there and get back to the compound ASAP. I ain't giving him nothing back, just going "yeah yeah" every thirty seconds.

"You all right up there, Willis?" he says to me just as we're entering the compound. "Don't seem like yourself today."

"I'm peachy," I say back. "Firin' on all cylinders."

By the time he'd released the slam locks on the back doors, I was waiting for him behind the truck. There was no one else in the compound, only me and Sherman and all that razor wire surrounding us. Herbert must have been in his office by then. I swear I could hear "Odin's Refrain" pounding in my head. Sherman gave me a stink-eyed look and took off toward the building.

All the while, I was thinking how much money half a million dollars was. I bet I could buy my Corvette and my AK47 with half a million dollars and still have some left over to travel the world. And then I remembered my plan: I was going to take that money and head to the southern lands until the heat went down. Or until I found a guild to join. It was like I was watching my own avatar in third-person mode, and he was doing shit that I never dreamed of.

Sherman was almost at the steel door at the back of the building when I pulled my Smith and Wesson and held the tip of the barrel two inches from the back of his head. He still had his bullet-proof vest on, so I knew a body shot wouldn't do no good. Sherman couldn't see what was happening behind him. He started to say something, and then I pulled the trigger.

Man, it was like in the middle of a game when everything all of a sudden goes slo-mo, and you hear the click of the hammer on the casing, and then there's blood all over the steel door, and you don't even hear the gun go off. It's like all you hear is this kind of baseline hum, the thing you hear when you walk into a hospital room and somebody's just died, but the heart monitor is still hooked up to him. Like on *House* or something. I didn't hear the gun go off, and I'm pretty sure Sherman didn't hear it either because he never screamed or anything. He just dropped like a zombie and bled out there on the asphalt.

He didn't die like he was supposed to, though. He kind of lay there and tried to get his breath, and then I turned him over, and I said, "Don't call me Willis anymore, okay?" And then he puked.

I picked up the satchel, and I left Sherman there like that, like he was wondering which realm he was in. I used my pass to get out of the compound, and then I got in my Kia Rio and drove away. The last thing I saw was Herbert coming out the back door into the compound and shouting something. He was looking around like he didn't know what to do. That's when I knew I'd beaten the game. I was in Level 110 or something, some level they hadn't even invented yet. Old Herbert would have to invent a whole new extension if he was going to beat me.

At least I did it with class. I terminated Sherman in the compound so his body was close to home. He wouldn't have to go to some spirit healer and beg for a resurrection. That's what I hope, anyway.

I kept hearing about me on the radio all the way down here. "Police are looking for Trevor Allan Blackmoor, twenty-four years old, Caucasian," the radio said. "Considered armed and dangerous." They didn't mention nothing about me being a Level 110 mage. It was like they were talking about somebody else. I couldn't recognize me.

And then, when I got down to the border, there were cop cars everywhere. Cops standing behind them with their guns drawn, waiting to unleash their full firepower against me. A good mage knows when to hold back and when to use his talents. I knew this was a time to hold back.

That's how I come to be talking to a bunch of Mounties right now, stuck in an eight-by-eight room on the Canadian side. Them talking about locking me up and throwing away the key.

But I ain't worried. I feel like I've been killed and resurrected a thousand times in my life already so maybe another resurrection is soon to come.

RESPITE

I FIRST MET Rory Ellison when he was still upright in bed, in the cold embrace of a prostate cancer that had spread to his lower spine and had searched with its spongy tentacles for his kidneys. He was remarkably coherent for a man so ill, sitting propped up against his pillows, wearing a smart set of light blue pyjamas and reading the *StarPhoenix*. Monogrammed with his initials, the pyjamas looked immaculate and unwrinkled, like they had been retrieved from the local dry cleaners earlier that day. He folded the newspaper when he saw me entering his bedroom and placed it gently on the lamp table beside his bed. His eyes were glassy from the morphine capsules he'd taken that morning, but he was otherwise alert. "Ah," he said, in that rich voice I'd heard a hundred times on the television, "the respite nurse. Who would have thought that Death could be so beautiful?"

It was an awkward moment. Twenty years ago, when my hair was a deep red and curly, I might have been insulted by an older man's attention. Now, as compliments for my looks were less frequent, I didn't mind hearing them so much. I was standing in the doorway with his wife, Barbara, a smartly dressed woman in her late sixties who, anyone could see, had been no slouch in the looks department herself. For my part, I have been quite used to patients commenting on my appearance, although it has nothing to do with what I am or what I've done. I didn't do anything to have an attractive face; I was merely born with it. As for my body, I can only say that men would be surprised by what they saw if I wasn't wearing any clothes.

Mrs. Ellison turned to me with a grim smile. "He's incorrigible," she said, "even at the ripe age of seventy-five."

"Don't tell her my age," her husband replied. "You'll scare her away."

I suppose I shouldn't have been surprised by his verve. He'd been a politician for thirty years, quite used to the give-and-take on the legislature floor. He had been a particular favourite of my father's; they shared the same political stripe, somewhat left of centre. My father used to say that Rory Ellison was the only politician he ever trusted because Rory Ellison was a friend of the common man. He had almost singlehandedly ramrodded a bill through the legislature that would pave the way for low-income housing in our major cities.

"I don't scare easy," I said, smiling at Mr. Ellison in what I hoped was a friendly but no-nonsense way. Even at his advanced age, I could see how someone might fall in love with him.

"Well," Mrs. Ellison said to me sharply, almost as though I were some kind of a threat. "You've seen the kitchen and the bathroom. You know where the pills are kept. Is there anything else I need to show you?"

"She knows everything she needs to know," Mr. Ellison interjected. He gave me that broad smile I'd seen in the newspapers. He had too many teeth for a man his age, and his grey wavy hair had been parted and combed immaculately.

I turned to Mrs. Ellison. "I'll be all right," I said. "Go and enjoy yourself." People think that respite is only about a delay before execution. More often than not, it's about an intercession in the taxing work of the caregiver.

"I'll have my cell phone with me," Mrs. Ellison said, "in case there are any problems."

When she had gone, Mr. Ellison grinned at me again. "I like to give her a hard time," he chuckled, "just so she knows I'm still alive."

"We haven't been properly introduced," I said. "My name is Joanna. Joanna McLeod." I shook his hand. The skin at the tips of his fingers was waxy and yellow, but he still had a hearty handshake.

"A Scottish lass," he trilled. "There are worse fates left for a man than to be cared for, on his deathbed, by a pretty Scottish lass." It was flirting, yes, but flirting in the harmless way that old men flirt with younger women.

"It's been a long time since anybody's called me a lass," I told him. That much is true. I've been called a bitch of late on more than one occasion but I haven't been called a lass. "I'm fifty years old."

"A spring chicken," he said, still smiling. He didn't bother to introduce himself. You'd have to live under a rock not to know who he was.

I sat in the chair beside the bed. "So tell me," I said, "how often do you take your meds?"

His smile evaporated. It was as if he'd forgotten his cancer the moment I'd walked in the door, and now I'd reminded him that he was sick. "As needed," he said drily. "Usually every three or four hours."

"I'm sorry if this is not the cheeriest conversation you've ever had," I said, "but I thought we should get it out of the way so that we can move forward." I wanted to establish a professional rela- tionship as early as possible.

His face had lost its animation for a moment. "That's fine,

then."

"I understand you've been catheterized," I said. "Any problems with that?"

Suddenly, he was grinning again. "You really cut to the chase, don't you, sister? No foreplay at all?"

I smiled back at him. "It's my job."

"You're talking about a tube they inserted in my dick," he said, "so I don't pee on my shoes."

"How's that been going for you?" I asked.

"Peachy."

You've got to be business-like in situations like this. "Any irritation?"

"Just when you remind me of it," he said, "or when I get an erection. Which hasn't been too often of late. Can we talk about something else?"

"What do you want to talk about?"

"Let's talk about love," he said. "Tell me about your love life."

I'm used to this from palliative care patients. They're commonly treated as diseased flesh, so they demand to be treated as people. "There's nothing to tell," I admitted.

He smiled devilishly. "Oh, come on. A beautiful young woman like you?"

I sat there for a moment, weighing the need to be honest against the need to maintain boundaries. *What the hell*, I decided. *I'm a little too old to play everything by the book.* "I'm in the middle of a divorce," I said.

TWO-THIRTY IN THE MORNING. The phone vibrated. The first line of "Another One Bites the Dust" played over and over. Benjamin.

I'd been in the apartment on Fourth Avenue for three

months, and I still woke up thinking I was in the house on Saskatchewan Crescent. I scrambled for the phone, only to realize that it was on the other side of the bed. Finally, after six or seven ringtones of the song, I picked up the receiver. "Yes?"

There was a brief pause, and then: "I miss you. I want you back."

"It's two-thirty in the morning."

"I miss you," he said more urgently.

"Don't call me anymore," I replied.

"Don't be like that," he said. Had he been drinking? "You know you're my only girl."

"No, Benjamin," I said, "I don't know that."

He took a deep breath, audible even over the phone. "I'll be the first to admit I've made mistakes," he said. "You're the one I love. Come back home."

"You knew what I was going through," I hissed into the phone. "You knew how vulnerable I was, and you did that."

"I didn't think," he replied.

"No. You didn't." I punched the end-call button on my phone and then went and poured myself a glass of water from the kitchen tap.

Thirty seconds later, the first line of Freddie Mercury's song played again. And again. And again. When it appeared Benjamin wasn't giving up, I picked up the phone.

"Why do you have to be like this?" he said. His voice was harder now.

"Like what?"

"Are you there with someone else?" Suddenly, he'd turned into his lawyerish self, cross-examining me.

"What if I am?"

"Is he there right now?"

"That's none of your business," I told him.

"Bitch," he hissed. "Fucking bitch."

I pressed the end-call button gently and switched off my phone. Then I went into the bathroom and found a sleeping pill.

A MONTH LATER, Mr. Ellison's condition had deteriorated sharply. He was no longer able to digest solid food. We kept him alive with porridge and potatoes and vegetables mashed up like baby food. The pain had nearly become unmanageable. After getting permission from his doctor, I increased the morphine dosage to one capsule per hour. Even the act of sitting him up in bed was a painful one. He uttered little cries with every adjustment. It was a stage of dying I recognized well: that time of life when the grown man reassumes the habits of a child, almost as if he's beginning to relearn the knowledge of immortality with which a child is born.

Of course, his catheter tube had not been kept clean in the intervening days since I last visited. Until that point, I was only hired to come in twice a week to give Mrs. Ellison a breather from her daily grind. There was major inflammation at the site where the catheter had been inserted into the penis. When I attempted to clean the infected area, Mr. Ellison made a brave attempt to deal with the pain. After a moment, I felt him shudder and begin to sob.

"Is this hurting you?" I said loudly, trying to break through the barriers the morphine had set up. "I can give you another pill if you would like." It wasn't time for another pill, but I figured an exception could be made.

He buried his face in his gnarled yellow fingers. "Don't touch me there!" he cried, as a five-year-old might. "Leave me alone!"

"I'm sorry, Mr. Ellison," I said, "but something has to be done, or this inflammation will get much worse."

"Don't touch me there!" he repeated.

"Okay," I said, "we'll leave it for now. But this catheter has to be managed." I went into the kitchen and dug up the ingredients for a wheat-germ smoothie.

When I returned to the bedroom, Mr. Ellison was lying on his side in a fetal position, facing the wall. "I'm going to sit you up now, Mr. Ellison," I said. "I've made you a nice drink." After much toing and froing, he was propped up against a pair of sturdy pillows. I held the glass to his mouth, and he drank the smoothie in measured sips. "I'm here for a few more hours," I said. "Is there anything else you'd like me to do?"

A small voice said, "You could read to me." He motioned toward the bedside table. "That book there."

There was a library copy of a novel called *The Moon and Sixpence* on the bedside table. It was bookmarked at Chapter 30, probably where Barbara had left off reading the day before. It was about a woman who had been unfaithful to her husband. "I was not much puzzled by Blanche Stroeve's action," I read, "for I saw in that merely the result of a physical appeal."

As I read further, I found myself remembering the news reports which had circulated, twenty years earlier, insinuating an affair between Rory Ellison and some young assistant in the legislature. The reports were from an era when newspapermen wrote cryptically about such things, when simply accusing a prominent politician of having an extramarital fling was not done. It had been easy, nevertheless, to sift through the suggestive language and find the subtext. I remembered reading how his wife had stood by him through denial after denial, and I began to understand that her possessiveness was probably rooted in that unseemly twenty-year-old suggestion, ultimately unproven, of an affair. I thought about all of this as the words flew by, page after page.

Through it all, Mr. Ellison remained sitting up in bed, his eyes closed as if concentration could ease the pain, moaning softly from time to time. I wasn't sure how much of my recitation he'd actually heard, but he seemed to be comforted by the sound of another voice, and so I kept reading. When I got to the part where Blanche killed herself, he lifted his hand tentatively from the bed covers, a gesture that meant I should stop. It was then that I could see tears rolling down his waxen face, and he said to me, again in a child-like voice, "Why do we do that to each other? Why do we hurt the people we love?"

A WEEK LATER, I was sitting in the boardroom of a law office in downtown Saskatoon. Not Benjamin's office. That would hardly be a neutral place. We were in the office of my lawyer, Al Livingstone, chosen for the fact that he was one of the best divorce lawyers in the city and also because my husband detested him.

I'd made a point of buying an expensive new business suit the week before, and I was sitting in a cushy leather chair next to Al. Benjamin had decided to show up in his usual blazer and tie, looking every inch the stuffed shirt that he'd become. He sat across the boardroom table from me and tried to be nonchalant.

"Good morning, Benjamin," Al said with a grin. No matter how well you dressed, you could never dress as well as Al. He wore $3,000 suits, tailor-made for him or bought in New York.

"Let's cut to the chase," Benjamin replied. "She wants the house and the car and the SUV and the cabin at Jackfish. She's not going to get them."

Al looked at me and smiled. "That's no way to start a negotiation," he said. "You know she's going to get the house, Benjamin. The woman always gets the house."

"Not always," Benjamin said. His jaw was set at a grim angle, and although his five o'clock shadow was evidence that he had not been taking care of himself, he seemed resolute. "Not this time."

He looked like he was ready to leap out of the chair and attack at any given moment.

Al reached into his briefcase and hauled out a ream of papers. "Okay, let's talk," he said. "I have here a list of all assets, both individual and combined."

"I've sold the house," Benjamin said quietly.

Al placed the papers on the table and stared unblinkingly at Benjamin. "You what?"

"I've sold the house. It's a done deal."

"You know we'll track the money," Al replied. "You can't hide it."

"We'll see," said Benjamin.

Something in me cracked at that moment. There we were, sitting in some plush law office boardroom with wood panel walls and photos of besuited former partners on them. Behaving like children. *I want this. You can't have that.* It was so far from the way I grew up, from the politics of my father, from my parents' marriage, which had lasted fifty-five years. It was so far from anything I'd ever wanted to be. I thought of Rory Ellison, lying on his death bed, a man who had given so much to his fellow men and who still lay there coming to terms with his own remorse. "A hundred thousand dollars," I heard myself say, "and the SUV."

The two men looked at me in disbelief. Finally, Benjamin shook his head. "What are you talking about?" he asked.

I looked at him squarely. "Give me a hundred thousand and the SUV," I said, "and we'll call it even." I suppose I could be accused of acting rashly. I wanted nothing more to do with Benjamin or his money. I wanted nothing more to do with love.

Al stared uncomprehendingly. "What are you saying?"

"I'm tired of all this," I replied. "I want out. This is my final offer."

"But you deserve so much more," Al said.

"That's all I want."

THE LAST TIME I saw Rory Ellison, he was lying in bed, his frail body tensed against the pain. Both he and his wife had insisted that he would die at home, if possible, with no tubes sticking out of him, no intravenous drip-feeding him.

When I arrived that morning, Mrs. Ellison looked almost as miserable as her husband. She had been up most of the night. Her blouse was wrinkled and unwashed, and her hair framed her once-pretty face in long stray wisps. "Poor dear," I said to her. "You should go back to bed."

Her response was terse. "I'm going to do some grocery shopping. I'll be back in a couple of hours."

When she had left, I went into Mr. Ellison's bedroom and sat down quietly in a chair beside the bed. He was lying on his back, breathing hoarsely, his mouth agape. His head had lost its handsomeness over the past month; it was little more than a skull covered with a taut parchment of yellow skin. He lapsed in and out of consciousness, groaning against the pain, mumbling unrelated words. I heard "Barbara" and "God" and "sorry."

After a few minutes, he came to with a startled jerk, gasping for air. I touched his feeble hand with mine. "It's all right," I whispered. "You can go if it's time to go."

He looked at me for a long time. His eyes were like deep, glassy ponds. "Hold me," he said in a small voice.

I'm not sure he even knew who I was. "Say that again," I whispered.

His eyes were pleading with me. "Please hold me." He squeezed my hand weakly.

It wasn't the best decision I've ever made, but I climbed up on the bed and lay down beside him. He was paper and wind, the walls of his chest like sheets of foolscap blowing around a parking lot. All I could think about was stopping the pain.

Whose pain?

"Hold me," he said.

I draped my arm across his skeleton of a body. He nestled his head into my neck. His breathing grew more relaxed. "I know how you feel," I whispered.

"No."

"Yes, I do." I took his aged hand and placed it where my left breast used to be. Do you feel that?"

"Gone?" he murmured.

"Yes," I said. "Cancer."

We lay, like two old lovers, for a long time. I'm not sure who was comforting whom. "Barbara," I thought I heard him murmur, and "Love." Then he came to with one more startled breath, his tortured abdomen jutting heavenward, exhaled the pain of his existence, and closed his eyes.

MEETING TIFFANY SLOANE

THERE SHE WAS, at last, a chiselled beauty, although fifty-five years old, her once tanned skin now clear and pale the way movie stars are these days with skin cancer on the rise. Her neck was swan-like, her lips in that pleasant pout he'd seen in all of her movies from *Indictment of Passion* to *Mount Vernon*. Her eyes were still piercing and intense.

Jack knew how rare these public appearances were, and he attributed this one to the fact that she hadn't had a hit movie in more than a decade. She had done the unexpected, Miss Sloane, and branched out into other work. This cookbook she was flogging was a case in point. Jack had read about it on her website, but he wasn't sure of the signals she was sending out. Did she consider her movie career over? Or was she a woman of passionate causes, and was yet another cookbook dedicated to vegetarian cuisine an expression of one of those causes?

"Never get too close to the illusion," Jack was fond of warning the tourists on his Hollywood tour. He wondered if he should have taken his own advice as he lined up in front of the ornate table at which Tiffany Sloane sat. Normally, he would have brought fifty eight-by-ten photographs to such an event, and he would have stood at that table until the star had signed every copy. To this event, he brought nothing, only his sixty-nine-year-old self and all his dreams in his trademark blue jeans and corduroy smoking jacket, his pencil moustache and his nose hairs neatly trimmed.

"Do you have a book for me to sign?" Her voice was polite and forward, with just the faintest hint of a Texas accent now, but there was no smile on Tiffany Sloane's still beautiful face. Had there been a facelift? If so, it was unusually successful; Jack couldn't tell.

Jack was lost in her piercing eyes. "A book?" he asked.

"You're supposed to pay for the book at the cashier's till," Tiffany Sloane said. "Then you're supposed to bring it here if you want me to sign."

THREE DAYS EARLIER, before he'd actually met his movie goddess, Jack had toured an eclectic busload of northerners through the Hollywood Hills. There had been an inordinate number of Canadians on the tour, many of them escaping what must have been the beginning of winter in the Great White North. One elderly couple declared that their daughter worked for the Toronto International Film Festival and that she'd phoned last spring to tell them she was standing ten feet away from Brad Pitt in the VIP lounge. *To hell with Brad Pitt*, Jack thought. *I'm showing you the authentic Hollywood right here.*

There was also a couple from Chicago on board. "I've heard," Jack said to them as they were waiting for the bus to fill, "that the South Side of Chicago is the baddest part of town. Is that correct?" The woman, a tough-looking broad in her own right, rolled her eyes and groaned. There were also some newlyweds from NYC, but Jack resisted the urge to belt out the chorus of "New York, New York," Ethel Merman style.

When the bus, a rickety old Chevrolet with a blue canvas canopy to protect the northerners from the sun, had filled, Jack slipped his hands-free microphone over his head, turned to his captive audience, and introduced himself. "Hi, folks, and welcome to the only official Hollywood Stars Tour, the tour that takes you everywhere and raises the curtain on some of Hollywood's most intimate moments. My name is Jack, and I will be your guide for the afternoon. And for the rest of your life." He waited for a laugh and got it. "Honestly," he said. "Your spiritual guide. This day will keep coming back to you in ways you can't imagine now. When you're in the shower. Or riding the subway. I'm your spiritual guide."

They were sitting on the corner of Las Palmas and Sunset Strip beside the old Baptist Church. Jack clunked the vehicle into gear and headed north toward Mulholland Drive. He pointed out the church hall where the dance scenes from *Back to the Future* were filmed and the fire escape that Richard Gere climbed to get to Julia Roberts at the end of *Pretty Woman*. "The City of Light!" Jack exclaimed. "Hollywood is all about what happens when light hits certain chemicals—something Richard Pryor learned to his everlasting regret. There's never been a shortage of chemicals in Hollywood."

Turning onto Mulholland Drive, he manoeuvred the bus up the steep, winding road to the lookout. "Believe it or not," he announced, "there have been frequent cougar sightings up here. And not just Cameron Diaz and J-Lo. Real cougars of the animal variety." He glanced at the passengers in the rear-view mirror. "But don't worry. They've only been known to attack Canadians wearing Tilley hats." At the back of the bus, the Canadian with the Tilley hat snorted, almost losing his false teeth.

Jack pulled into the parking area by the Hollywood sign lookout. "That's the famous Hollywood sign over there," he said. "It fell into disrepair in the 1970s when the H slid down the hill. In the 1990s, my own personal hero, Hugh Hefner, paid for the restoration of the sign. So, you see, Hugh is not just my own personal hero but the saviour of all Hollywood." Jack waited patiently while the tourists' cameras clicked and whirred and their iPhones did whatever iPhones did.

Then he steered the bus back onto the road and headed toward Quentin Tarantino's lofty mansion. "Quentin," he said, "doesn't like to be asked for autographs." What the tourists really wanted, and what they almost never got, was a sighting of one of the stars. Jack felt it necessary to regale them with fictitious sightings on past tours. "It's a pity Uma Thurman isn't out today. On locals-only day three weeks ago, she stopped us and asked if we wanted to take pictures."

They wound back down the hill, past Sasha Baron Cohen's house with the Tree of Life on his gate. A cop was waiting around a hairpin curve. He yelled at Jack through his open window. "Do you wanna ticket?"

"Nope."

"Keep moving, then. I don't want any of these people killed in a rear-end collision."

"Yes, officer," Jack replied, but when he was turning down Laurel Canyon Road and the cop was well and truly out of earshot, he muttered, "Yes, asshole," into his microphone. The tourists chuckled. "Just another day in paradise!"

Jack regaled them all with the old joke about the guy whose job it was to clean the elephant's cage in the circus. Because they were in close quarters, the elephant was always shitting on the guy's head. When asked why he didn't simply quit his job, the guy retorted, "What? And give up show business!"

Down into Beverly Hills they rode, near the place where poor old Monty Clift crashed his car on the way home from a party at

Liz Taylor's house. Monty had wandered through a half dozen movies after that with a shell-shocked look on his once-perfect face. Past Hugh Hefner's famous mansion (no Hugh on the lawn in his pyjamas today, no frisky Playmates) they went, past Ellen Degeneres's former home and down Roxbury Avenue, home of the old-time stars and Lucille Ball's domestic-looking house. "I think you have some 'splaining to do, Lucy," Jack shouted, doing his spot-on impression of Desi Arnaz.

Jack always hated the tail end of his tour, especially on days when nothing out of the ordinary happened. It was just depressing, and lately, depression had gotten the best of him. They drove down Rodeo Drive. "Come down here tomorrow with about thirty thousand dollars, ladies," he said. "That'll buy you about three dresses." He noticed a tall black man in his rear-view mirror as they passed Gucci. "Look!" he called feverishly. "It's Wilt Chamberlain. Everybody shout hello to Wilt!" The passengers craned their necks to see Wilt or somebody who looked like him, disappearing in the distance. "Oh, look, a Lamborghini," Jack said, distracting them. "It goes three hundred miles per hour. For those days when you need to go three hundred miles per hour."

Past the Viper Club they went, where River Phoenix met his untimely end. "Light and chemicals," Jack reiterated tragically. "The coroner said he overdosed on a mixture of heroin, crystal meth, ecstasy, and rainbow skittles." And no tour would be complete before they drove past Whisky-A-Go-Go and the Château Marmont, where some Canadian chick shot up John Belushi the night he died.

AFTER A TOUR, Jack always needed a shower. He parked the bus in front of his building on Cochran Avenue and trudged up three sets of stairs to his apartment.

Jack could hear strains of "Stairway to Heaven" as he opened the door, and he surmised that he'd forgotten to turn the bedside radio off before he left that morning. There was still a burnt offering of toast on the small kitchen table, but the studio apartment was as he had left it, glossy eight-by-tens of all his favourite stars Scotch-taped to the plasterboard walls like holy icons and false idols. The famous picture from *Reservoir Dogs* was there, all the besuited actors walking toward the camera. Marilyn, over the grate, her skirt rising gleefully in the under-draft, giggled enigmatically as she incurred the wrath of Arthur Miller. Sophia Loren glanced disapprovingly at Jayne Mansfield's décolletage in another photo, and, of course, Jean Seburg cavorted in a Roman fountain as the paparazzi begged her to look at them.

Near his bed, though, was Jack's shrine to Tiffany Sloane, lit by two electric candles that never burned out. There were stills from *Indictment of Passion*, *Haunted Holiday*, and six of her other movies, but Jack's favourite photo was an eight-by-ten from Tiffany's modelling years. He had ordered it from her website ten years earlier and had paid twenty-five dollars for a personalized autograph. "For Jack," it said, "a fellow traveller on Life's Highway. With Love, Tiffany Sloane."

Jack paused before Tiffany's photo, as he always did, and began to undress. *She might be fifty-five years old*, he thought, *but I'd still do her*. Naked at last before his celluloid goddess, Jack glanced down at his half-erect penis. "Wouldn't need Cialis for that, would we? Nosirree Bob."

He chuckled to himself, remembering that she would be launching her new book in three days, and sauntered off to his bathroom for a long, hot shower.

JACK SLEPT RESTLESSLY THAT NIGHT, dreaming that recurring dream where he was begging for money on the Sunset Strip. Usually, he was kicked and prodded by LAPD's finest in his dream, but that night, something different happened. Tiffany Sloane walked by, flanked by a bodyguard and her fat husband. She insisted on stopping, although the burly bodyguard wanted her to move on. "I know this man," she said. "He asked for my picture and my autograph some time ago." Against the remonstrations of her husband and her bodyguard, she knelt down beside Jack, next to Fatty Arbuckle's star in the Walk of Fame, and cradled his head in her lap.

An insistent buzz from the downstairs intercom woke Jack from his reverie. He stumbled to the phone in his briefs and almost lost his balance when he picked up the receiver. "What?" he snapped. Drug addicts were always pressing the buzzer, trying to get into the air-conditioned building and out of the oppressive heat.

"It's me," his daughter droned. "Let me in."

Jack got himself dressed in jeans and a wife-beater in time for his daughter's entrance. She was standing at the door in her Denny's uniform, waving a lit cigarette at him. Smoking, Jack thought, had ruined her appearance. "Maisie," he said, "it's nice to see you."

Maisie stood at the door and peered witheringly at Jack's dark apartment. "I can't stay long," she said. "I've got to be at the restaurant in half an hour." They stared at each other uncomfortably for a few seconds, and Maisie spoke again. "I talked to Mom like you said, but she's not willing to help out."

"She's got the money," Jack replied.

"I know she's got the money. She's married to a goddamn optometrist, for Christ's sake."

Jack looked brokenly at his daughter. "Why don't you come in and sit down?"

"You're my only hope, Dad. If you could just free up a thousand dollars."

"I don't have a thousand dollars." Jack tried to look poverty-stricken, which wasn't too difficult in his soiled undershirt.

Maisie's voice got hard. "You could sell some of your memorabilia."

Jack couldn't believe what he was hearing. "Sell my memorabilia?" he almost shouted. "So Rory can snort the profits up his nose?"

"He's not gonna snort the goddamn profits," Maisie shouted back. Her breathing was laboured, and Jack thought for a moment that she was going to throw her lit cigarette at him. She took a deep breath and seemed to calm down. "He's clean. He needs the money to start his remodelling business."

"I'm sorry." Jack busied himself pouring coffee grounds into the filter on his coffee maker.

Maisie took another step into the room. "Please, Dad," she said, adopting the insistent beggarly tones of her drug-user boyfriend. "I'll never ask you for another loan again. I promise."

Jack sat at the kitchen table, rubbing his left hand over his face.

"Please, Dad," she said.

He looked at the ceiling. "I can give you five hundred today," he heard himself say, "and five hundred next month."

BY THE TIME Jack had purchased Tiffany Sloane's book, the lineup in front of her desk had begun to dissipate. *Good,* Jack thought, fingering the glossy cookbook. *Maybe she'll have time to chat.*

"You bought the book," Tiffany Sloane said to him as he edged up to her table.

"Yeah."

She looked Jack straight in the eye. "Do you cook your own meals?"

"When I don't eat in restaurants," Jack said. She had a way of putting a guy at ease.

"That's very good, then." She picked up a pen in her left hand. She was left-handed. Jack wondered how that fact had escaped him all these years. "To whom shall I sign it?"

Jack stared at her uncomprehendingly. At last, he said, "My name is Jack."

"For Jack, then." She wrote something on the title page of the cookbook, right underneath *Sexy Veggie Dishes for Food Lovers*, and handed the book back to him.

"I was wondering," Jack blurted, "if you'd like to have a cup of coffee with me sometime."

Tiffany Sloane took his invitation in stride as though she'd had many more like it and had turned them all down. "Ah, that's very sweet of you, Jack. But I'm a married woman, you see. With a busy schedule of personal appearances."

Jack wondered what he could have been thinking. "No, of course," he said, trying to regain his composure. "What I meant was, could I get you a cup of java from the Starbucks over there? I'd go get it for you."

Tiffany Sloane smiled at him. "I'm in the midst of a cleanse at the moment," she said, "or I'd take you up on that offer."

Jack worried that the conversation was over. "I—I—I—" he stammered. "I'm your biggest fan."

She eyed him with a mixture of pity and compassion. "Do you live in Los Angeles, Jack?"

"Yes, down in Malibu."

"You look like a prime candidate for my personal workshop on self-improvement," she said. "It'll be offered next month."

"Oh?"

Tiffany Sloane folded her hands in front of her like a politician. "I guess I can tell you about it," she said, "since there's no lineup at the moment. We use techniques in movie acting to improve the self-concept. You're given circumstances. Objectives. Obstacles. Then, we collaborate on a set of characteristics you want to adopt. The whole thing culminates with a big party at a hotel in Marina Del Rey, where you will unveil the new character you've become."

"What's the cost?" Jack asked blankly.

"Only four hundred and ninety-five dollars."

MAISIE WAS NOT happy when she heard that Jack wasn't coming through with his second instalment of the money. She threw a hissy fit right there at his door, threatening to disown him. "Honest to God," she shouted, "I have the most dysfunctional parents on the planet!"

Staring down at his breakfast as Maisie berated him, Jack secretly wished to be transported to another place and time. He could think of no response that would satisfy her, so he just sat there in his underwear and studied the moon-like contours of the bread. Finally, Maisie walked out the door, slamming it behind her with a resounding thud. Jack heard her shout, "Fuck you!" as she stomped down the corridor to the stairwell.

He remained at the kitchen table for a moment, contemplating the vicissitudes of his sad life. Like a shoveller of shit in the circus, Jack worked hard for his money. Ferrying goddamn tourists around the Hollywood Hills for a hundred bucks a day was no picnic. It took its toll on a man, all that hocus pocus about movie stars who were his close personal friends. Even so, he couldn't bring himself to retire.

After he'd choked down his toast, Jack straggled into the bathroom. He took a dump, showered, and shaved. Tampering with his comb-over in the bathroom mirror, he thought for a brief, shining moment that he didn't look too bad for an old man who'd been baked in the California sun for forty years. He went into the bedroom and donned a pair of black slacks. He squeezed into the smoker's jacket that he'd liberated from an antique clothing shop several years before.

When he arrived at the self-improvement seminar, Jack noticed that most of the other participants were men and women of a certain age. Better dressed and more suave than Jack, they stood in the lobby of the Marina Del Ray hotel, jabbering about Tiffany Sloane and her movies. A young man sat at a desk near the door of the convention room, collecting the $495 entrance fee as people filed past him.

Inside the convention room, the attendees sat on uncomfortable folding chairs, waiting for the movie star's entrance. At ten o'clock precisely, a curtain opened at the front of the room, revealing a large projection screen. The image flickered for a moment, and then Tiffany Sloane came into view. Jack had fully expected Miss Sloane to be there in person, and he groaned audibly when he realized that she would not be present. Elsewhere in the room, others expressed their displeasure in a similar fashion.

Tiffany Sloane was sitting at a desk in front of a computer screen somewhere, probably in her own mansion. Translucent as always, she welcomed her paying audience. "When I played Alma Schlesinger in *Indictment of Passion*," she began, "I had to imagine the given circumstances of my character. I started with the fact that she was unhappily married. She also had a child who depended on her. And a would-be lover, her husband's best friend, who gave her the attention she so desperately needed." She paused and looked meaningfully into the camera, into the souls of the men and women who had assembled to see her. It struck Jack that she was still quite beautiful without the benefits of a makeup artist and studio lighting, even as she was Zooming them from her own computer. "Now I want you all to find a pen and a piece of paper," Tiffany Sloane continued, "and I want you to write down the ten given circumstances of your own lives."

Scribbling feverishly at a piece of paper in front of him, Jack struggled to be honest with himself. "Divorced," he wrote. "On the poverty line. A daughter who bleeds me dry."

To fill the void while everybody was busy writing, Tiffany Sloane spoke up again. "Over the course of the day," she said, "you will develop a character that is capable of fighting against these crippling given circumstances. That character will be the new you."

The woman next to him sneezed, which irritated Jack. He glanced at her as she resumed writing. She was dressed like Tiffany Sloane in *Mount Vernon*: white blouse and pencil skirt. Her skin was taut and pale, and her brunette hair swept across her forehead like an accident that was somehow meant to be. "Take a picture," the woman said. "It'll last longer."

"I didn't mean to stare," Jack said. "It's just that you look like . . ."

"Yeah, I know," she replied. "I look like Tiffany."

On the projection screen at the front of the room, the real Tiffany Sloane was urging them on. "The sky's the limit," she intoned. "You can be anybody you want to be."

Jack thought about that for a second. If you could be anybody you wanted to be, why was there only one Tiffany Sloane? He turned to the woman beside him. "Do you believe that?"

"If I didn't," she said, "I wouldn't be here."

Jack shook his head. "Light and chemicals."

The woman gave him a death stare. "What's that supposed to mean?"

On the screen, Tiffany Sloane continued speaking. Her voice

sounded tinny now, and her face was a garish bright green. Jack put it down to bad lighting, a cheap sound system, and a terrible internet connection. "At the end of the workshop today, you will be encouraged to enrol in a more advanced session that I call 'Lessons from the sound stage: the art of living in the moment.'"

WHEN JACK GOT BACK to his apartment, it was only five-thirty in the afternoon but already pitch-dark. He didn't bother to turn on the lights. He sat at his kitchen table and looked at the shrine to Tiffany Sloane above his bed. The phone rang again and again, but he did not answer it.

And then, at half past eleven, he methodically removed Tiffany Sloane's eight-by-tens from his wall, placed them in a file folder, and tucked them away in his sock drawer. He unplugged the electric candles for the first time in fifteen years.

He showered and went to bed, switching on the bedside lamp. Tiffany Sloane's cookbook, which had cost him $21.95 a month earlier, was sitting on the night table. Jack opened the book to its title page and found exactly the same dedication he had received on the photograph Sloane's website had sent him years earlier. "For Jack," it read right under the subtitle. "A fellow traveller on Life's Highway. With Love, Tiffany Sloane."

TWO DAYS LATER, Jack was on the road again, ferrying a group of European tourists through the Hollywood Hills. Half of them didn't speak English, so Jack curtailed his usual spiel, limiting himself to pointing at signs and buildings and reciting place names. He pointed and said, "Mulholland Drive," and then "the Hollywood sign," and then "Quentin Tarantino's house."

He wondered if the tourists understood a word of what he was saying, but partly, he was beyond caring. As he steered the large, open van, his mind drifted to thoughts of light and chemicals, but now the light seemed far in the distance, and the chemicals were little more than a chimera of mercury and mirrors.

As they passed Sasha Baron Cohen's mansion, Jack heard a muffled pop that sounded like a balloon bursting. His van swerved on the asphalt, and he pulled to a stop on the side of the road at one end of the hairpin curve. After jumping down from the driver's seat, he saw that his rear tire was little more than a tattered rag of rubber. "Fucking Vernon," he muttered to himself. "Calls himself a mechanic, but he can't keep these vehicles in working order." He found a jack in the back of the vehicle and slid it under the frame behind the rear axle. He didn't bother to order his passengers off the van.

He was still muttering profanities when a security guard from one of the nearby properties approached him. "The hell you doin' here?" the security guard asked. His voice was hard, and when Jack turned to look at him, it was clear that he was a hard man all around, about six-foot-four with a pair of tattooed forearms that seemed to burst out of his long-sleeved shirt.

"It's a public roadway," Jack replied. "I guess we have as much right to be here as you do."

The security guard hovered over him. "I'll give you five minutes to get this heap out of the driveway. After that, your ass is grass."

Jack was formulating a witty reply when a car came veering around the tight curve. He did not see the kid who was driving the car, did not see the gleam of the California sun off its grill. He heard a screech of tires and the hollow thud of metal on metal, and he felt the tremor as the car's front bumper smashed into the rear of the van. And then he was splayed over a curb at the side of the road, and his entire body hurt and the security guard was nowhere in sight. The last thing he heard before passing out was the moaning of one of his passengers, soft and low in the summer heat, a tortured keening that was intelligible in any language.

He could have sworn that Tiffany Sloane came to him then. She knelt down and cradled his throbbing head in her lap, and before the lights went out, he looked into her eyes and saw that she was smiling beatifically, and he was comforted in the knowledge that the world was unfolding as it should.

ISLA MUJERES

STILL IN HIS PYJAMAS, my husband Jim is stretched out on one of a pair of beds, a rum and Coke in his hand. Our friends, Nancy and Don, are lounging on the comfy sofa, looking slightly more dignified in their shorts and tee shirts. We've been at the Plaza Royale resort in Playa del Carmen for a couple of days now, and it's almost ten o'clock on a Tuesday morning. "Don't know why she wants to go down to the beach at this hour," Jim mutters, "when there's all the free booze you can drink right here in the resort."

"I want some fresh air on this trip," I say, coming out of the bathroom with my bathing suit on, a nice one-piece I bought back in Saskatoon. I'm still in pretty good shape for a fifty-year-old, with all the running and workouts at the gym, but I think I've passed the expiry date for a bikini. "We didn't come to Mexico to sit in the room and drink, did we?"

At least Nancy's on my side. "Julie's right," she says. "We came here for the weather, and we should enjoy it."

"I booked a sailboard lesson last night," I tell them, taking one last look at myself in the mirror. "You guys should stay here and enjoy the pool or whatever. I'll be back in a couple of hours."

"Suit yourself," Jim replies, with a vague wave of his hand, "but there's more fun to be had here with us." He reaches over to the bedside table to pick up his glass, but he accidentally knocks it over onto the carpet. "Oh, shit, guess I better pour myself another."

I remember when I was a kid taking swimming lessons back at Day's Beach. My dad warned me not to try and rescue a drowning person. "They'll pull you under with them," he said. "They're that desperate."

"Don't worry about a thing, Julie," Nancy interjects. "I'll get these big galoots moving, and we'll be down there in time to watch your lesson."

"See you down there, then, in a few minutes." I pull the door shut behind me and feel a wave of Caribbean heat on my skin. It feels good to be out of the room.

I'M STANDING in fine white sand as Hector explains how you get on the board once you're in the water and how you pull up the sail. He wonders if I'll have enough strength once I'm out there. I tell him I'm stronger than I look, but he says he isn't sure. He wraps a large brown hand around my shoulder. Does the promise of a flirtation with a much younger man come with the sailboard lesson? "Perhaps," he says, his accent thick as the sand between my toes, "perhaps you do have the strength." He smiles. "You must wear a life vest, just in case. *Claro?*"

"Yes." He hands me the life vest. I'm surprised that he doesn't try to zip it up for me.

"There is a beach party here tonight," he says. "Will you come?"

"I might."

"Is fun. Dancing." He mimes a little salsa. He must be about twenty-five. My son at home is almost that old. "You are ready, yes?"

"What?"

"You are ready to try this out in the water. Yes?" He brushes the long hair out of his eyes and smiles again. "I think you are ready."

Then we are in the water. He clasps two hands around my waist and helps me up on the board. He holds my hand as I come to a standing position.

"Very good," he says. "Now, I let go of your hand, and you balance." He releases my hand, and I belly-flop into the water.

After a few more attempts, I notice Nancy and Don watching from the shore. Jim is nowhere to be seen. Nancy waves and shouts something, but I can't hear her over the sound of the Caribbean washing in. I wave back.

"You must be one with the sea, *senorita*," Hector says. He insists on calling me *senorita*, although the wedding ring on my hand announces that I'm a *senora*.

"I've been one with the sea about five times now," I say with a laugh. "I've swallowed about a gallon of water."

"Yes," he says, "but you must feel the sea in your feet and in your knees and in your belly."

I try to imagine how to put this sage piece of advice to use, but I can't. I like facts and numbers, not metaphors.

Hector holds the board while I stand on it. "Now pull!" he shouts, and I pull the sail out of the water. There is a moment of indecision when the wind doesn't know what to do, and then the plastic sail billows and I'm off! It's easy once you're standing, once the lesson is learned. I glide through the water like I know what I'm doing, gradually straightening up and relaxing. "Don't go far from shore, *senorita*," shouts Hector. "That way, I can swim out and help you."

It's too late for that, though. I'm past the waves, out on the glassy turquoise. Nancy and Don are jumping up and down and cheering. I lean backward, into the wind, and I'm not sailing anymore. I'm flying, flying in a cloudless turquoise sky.

I READ a magazine article about drowning once—maybe it was in *Shape* or *Muscle and Fitness*—about how it feels when your lungs fill up with water and you surrender to it. Apparently, there's a kind of euphoria that you experience as the brain is gradually depleted of oxygen. I imagine that euphoria to be like drunkenness. It wouldn't be the worst way to die.

It's four in the afternoon, and I've found a chair in the lobby where I can answer my emails. There are a few from my work at the bank that I ignore. What part of "I will be away from the office until December 21" do they not understand? I scroll through the junk mail until I find a message from Richard. He's sent me a YouTube link to a song. It's "Fields of Gold," but I can't stream it in a place where the internet is spotty.

Richard's emails are predictable. He will never get down and dirty. He opts instead for romanticism. He is the most romantic real estate agent I've ever met. It's hard to be without romance in your life. *How's the playa?* he writes. *Meet any handsome Mexican cabana boys?*

Richard is convinced that I've come down here to Mexico in order to rekindle my marriage. I suppose I could hope for that, but if I'm truthful, I've come down here out of loyalty to Nancy and Don. And to Jim, too, I suppose. We've vacationed together in Mexico for the last ten years, and this particular trip was planned before Jim did what he did to my father.

I don't know why I carry on with this email flirtation. *It's harmless*, I tell myself. *We aren't sleeping together.* I suppose I crave the attention of men.

There's something vulnerable about Richard, even when he drives his expensive SUV and pounds real estate signs into people's front lawns. He's drowning, too, I suppose, smothered in a passionless marriage but staying for the sake of his children. Come to think of it, he might also be staying for his own sake because he actually enjoys the experience of drowning or because he is in love with appearances. He sells the appearance of a happy home and part of that sales pitch is seeming happy himself.

Enjoying the sun and the sand, I type into my iPad. *Might go for a massage later. Thinking of you, Julie.* I hit send just as Nancy approaches.

"There you are!" she says. "We were wondering where you disappeared to."

JIM IS CURLED up on the bed, cradling an almost empty bottle of rum between his arms, when I get back to the room. He awakens when he hears me turn on the shower. "Is that you?" he says in that low growl that comes out of his mouth when he's been drinking a lot.

"Yes, it's me." I slip out of my sundress as he's coming around the divider and the two-person Jacuzzi. He's still wearing his pyjamas, still cuddling his bottle. "You should shave and get dressed," I say. "Nancy and Don are meeting us for supper at seven."

"You can't just ignore me this entire vacation," he says.

"You looked like you wanted to be alone."

His eyes are red. "Don't make a point of embarrassing me in front of our friends."

"You embarrass yourself," I say, turning my back so I can unhook my bra.

An empty whisky bottle sails past my head and smashes the mirror in front of me. I don't even have time to scream. I can't quite catch my breath as I see the mirror broken in haphazard shards. Then, just as suddenly, I feel dead inside. The only way to deal with Jim when he gets like this is to stand up to him.

"Are you going to try and hurt me now?" I shout. "Are you going to slap me around a little? Or do you save that kind of treatment for eighty-five-year-old men?"

For a moment, I think he might actually do it, coil his shaking hand into a fist and lash out at me. I'd be relieved if he did. There would be nothing more to keep me in this relationship.

There is a vacancy in Jim's eyes as he fumbles around the room for a chair and sits in it. "I never meant to hit your father," he hisses. "It was an accident."

"It was no accident," I say, taking the offensive. "He wouldn't lend you the money, and so you hit him."

"I did it for you," he says quietly. "For our family. I needed that money to keep the firm afloat." Then Jim is crying fierce tears that roll down his cheeks like waterfalls. He rubs his palms against his eyes as if trying to push his eyeballs through the back of his head. As if trying to stop the tide from coming in. He looks up at me. "I've never walked away from trouble in my life. You know that, Julie."

"I know."

"And I think that walking away from this marriage would be a real admission of failure." His voice has lost its edge now.

I'd like to touch him, to run my hand through his hair, but I can't. "I have to shower," I say. "We're meeting Don and Nancy in an hour."

LUCKILY, Don and Nancy are quite talkative at supper because Jim doesn't say a word. Don loads up at the smorgasbord, all the while spouting off about this kid who tried to sell him black-market Viagra in the village. "Do I look like I can't get it up?" he asks. Nancy laughs and rolls her eyes.

We're staying in a five-star all-inclusive, but you wouldn't know it by looking at Jim's plate. Three pieces of calamari and a little pasta are all he eats.

After supper, Don and Nancy head off to their room. Jim says he's tired and wants to sleep. I tell him I want to look at some of the resort shops. He walks back to the room alone.

At nine o'clock, I stroll down to the beach. I've been warned that it's dangerous for a woman to go down to the beach alone after dark, but places like this are always more dangerous by reputation than they are when you actually get there. Besides, there's safety in numbers.

Someone has strewn patio lanterns along the eaves of the wedding pagoda, and there are more lights along the roofline of the beachside bar. There are Mexicans here as well as tourists. Music is blaring from one of those boom boxes that looks like an electric generator. It plays a samba version of "Feliz Navidad." One of the hotel workers is leading a samba lesson on the sand, a lesson taken mostly by hopeful-looking twenty-something girls wearing bikini tops and short skirts. The hotel worker shouts instructions into a megaphone, admonishes the tourist girls to shake their *cuelos*. Mostly young men stand at the bar in their board shorts and short-sleeved shirts. They knock back mojitos like there's no tomorrow.

I feel decidedly overdressed in my Capri pants and light sweater and about twenty-five years too old for this crowd. I watch the dancing for a few minutes and then turn to go back to the resort, back to my room, where Jim is probably drunk asleep by now.

Hector is leaning on the railing of the footbridge as I approach. He watches me appreciatively, and then, as I'm about to pass, he smiles at me. "Miss Julie," he says, "you came to the beach party."

"Only to see what was happening," I say.

He looks deep into my eyes, a long, soulful look that I imagine he's practised on many tourist girls in the past. "Don't like what you see?"

"It's not so much what I see but what I hear," I say. "The music's too loud."

"Perhaps we should go for a walk down the beach," he says, "where it will be quieter." He has his hand on the sleeve of my sweater now, toying with it the way men do when they don't know how else to touch you.

"I think I should go back," I say.

"Are you afraid of me?" His voice is even and assured.

"No." How can I be afraid of him? He's just a kid.

"Well, then." His other hand is on the small of my back now, and I think how much more enjoyable this is than going back to my sleeping husband. I also think how embarrassed I would be if Don and Nancy strolled over the bridge at this moment.

"Okay," I say. "Let's go for a walk."

Hector takes my hand and leads me off the bridge, turning quickly to the right so we can avoid the partyers. We pick our way among the grass beach umbrellas. The music from the beach party recedes into the background, and the sound of the waves is once again relentless. At last, we are alone in the moonlight.

"Do you know what I think?" he asks.

"What?"

"I think we should kiss," he says, putting his arm around my waist.

I push him away. "You're very nice," I say, "and very young."

His brown eyes glisten in the darkness. "I am a man," he says simply.

We look at each other for a long time. Then I tell him I have to go.

ON THE WAY back to the resort, I find a piece of paper in the pocket of my Capris. It's a note I wrote to myself when the trouble with Jim got out of control about a year ago. I stop under a light on the walkway and read it. "Think of H = Love," it says. "Loved him/felt loved/loved his family deeply." I smile at my own mathematical precision. H equals Hal, my high school sweetheart, equals love. You can't quantify love; you only know when it's there and when it isn't.

When I get back to the room, Jim is explaining to a Mexican caretaker how the mirror above the sink came to be broken. "Slipped coming out of the shower," he slurs, "and I banged my head against it."

The caretaker doesn't speak much English. He looks back and forth between the broken mirror and Jim and grins. "Your head? Is okay?"

"Yeah," Jim says. "I didn't even get a scratch."

I sit on my bed, and Jim sits on his, while the handyman meticulously takes down the wreckage that once was a mirror. We watch Mexican baseball on the flat-screen television. Jim pours himself a drink and falls asleep before the caretaker finishes.

WE LEAVE IN TWO DAYS, back to the polar freeze, and I'm lounging in the hotel foyer, answering my emails. Richard is getting more and more cloying. *Life is hell without you*, he writes.

Hurry home please. He sends me another YouTube URL, this one for Bruce Cockburn's "Coldest Night of the Year."

I imagine him sitting down to breakfast at this moment with his wife and family. They are all very civil, but Richard is quiet. They discuss school and friends and the Christmas holidays. They live in a pretty house on Saskatchewan Crescent.

We need to talk when I get home, I find myself writing. I don't really know why I want to send that message, but I do.

I flip the cover on my iPad as Nancy approaches. "I'm always finding you here," she says.

"The internet's faster here than in the room," I tell her.

"Or maybe you're avoiding Jim?"

Our eyes meet. It's the first time she's confronted the subject head-on. "You think so?"

"Oh, come on, Julie," she says, putting her hand on mine. "It's written all over your face." Nancy runs a hair salon; she's not as in love with facts and numbers as I am, but she's more intuitive.

I try to be nonchalant. "What's written all over my face?"

"That you're leaving him."

I take a deep breath. "No."

"You've left him already," she says. "You just don't know it yet."

"No."

"Look, it's none of my business," Nancy replies. "I just want you to know that, whatever happens, I will always be your friend."

We talk for a while longer, but then Don strolls into the lobby wearing orange Bermuda shorts. I'm almost blinded by their brightness. "I know," Nancy says. "I told him not to buy them, but he doesn't listen."

"You ladies coming for breakfast?" Don asks, with a smile as broad as a Mexican sunrise.

"I don't know if I want to be seen with you in that get-up,"

Nancy says. "Maybe I'll take a table off in a corner somewhere by myself."

"How about you, sister?" Don says, casting an imaginary hook at me and reeling me in.

"I'll be down in a minute," I tell him. "Just a few more emails to answer."

After they've gone, I flip open the iPad again. There's a message from the office. *I need some particulars on the Flaherty account*, my boss writes. I don't write back. The Flaherty account can wait until I sort out my life.

IT'S our last full day in Playa del Carmen, and I'm reclining under a grass umbrella at the beach, pondering the future. I've never been without a man in my life. I was always Daddy's little girl, the tomboy who played football on the school grounds just like my brothers. Then there was Hal, and that left me shaken when we finally broke up. I met Jim when we were at university, both of us in Commerce. He was a bright young man then, full of joy, full of jokes. We got married as soon as we graduated, had two children and a house in Erindale. Then came the worries about one of Jim's apartment complexes, and the drinking started.

The waves crash in relentlessly, and the sun is high in the sky. I don my sunglasses and pick up a book, Bill Gaston's *Juliet Was a Surprise*. I'm ensconced in a story entitled "To Mexico" when Hector strides into my field of vision.

"*Buenos dias, senorita*," he says. He's wearing only his board shorts and a pair of sandals.

"I'm not a *senorita*," I say. "Look, here's my ring."

He sits on the beach chair next to me. "No, but you should be a *senorita*," he says. "It suits you."

I look over my sunglasses at him. "Aren't you afraid my husband is going to come down here and kick your ass?"

He shrugs his muscular shoulders. "I have never met your husband. Why should he want to kick my ass?"

"He would want to if he knew what you were trying to do to me."

He rests a brown hand on my ankle like a gesture of this sort is nothing, like it's just the way things are done in Mexico. "Perhaps," he says, gazing steadily into my eyes.

I kick his hand away, get up off the chair. "I can't do this."

"Why not?"

"Because it's wrong."

"There is nothing wrong," Hector tells me, his voice even. "There is only what you do and what you don't do."

I think I've heard that line in a movie somewhere. I look around to see if Don and Nancy are nearby. They aren't. "In any case," I say to Hector, "I'm not going to do this." I gather my book and my beach towel and throw them into a shoulder bag.

Hector tries to call me back, but I'm already halfway down the beach.

THERE'S a problem with our tickets at the airline counter in Cancun. For some reason, Jim has been booked into a seat in Row C while I have been booked in Row L. Nancy and Don, who booked through a different travel agent, are seated together.

Jim sits in the gate lounge with his briefcase and his clear plastic bag of duty-free Scotch at his feet. He's fuming at our travel agent back home. Nancy and Don have gone off to the tourist shop to buy a few trinkets. "It's no big deal," I say to Jim. "We've had these mix-ups before."

"And it's about time they stopped," Jim snaps. He retrieves

his phone from the briefcase and punches in a bunch of numbers. "Hello, Helen," he says, his voice flooded with irony. "Julie and I are sitting at the airport in Cancun. You can imagine our surprise when we learned that we weren't booked into the same row." He listens for a moment, and then his voice drops an octave. "*I* was supposed to do that? *I* was supposed to do that? Well, if *I* was supposed to do that, maybe next time, *I'll* just book my own tickets from the get-go." Heads are starting to turn because he's almost yelling. He punches the phone blindly again, fires it into his briefcase, and sits there like a volcano that's about to erupt.

"There's no need to be rude to Helen," I say.

"It's getting to be a pretty fucking sad time," Jim fumes, "when a man can't sit on an airplane next to his wife."

"I don't love you anymore," I say, and I can't believe what I'm hearing from my own mouth.

The blood drains from Jim's face. "Huh?"

"I don't love you anymore," I say as plainly as I can.

THERE'S something about flying that makes you clear-headed and precise. The worlds of land and ocean fall away the farther you ascend into the sky, and you begin to see what matters. I look out of my window in Row L and observe the turquoise water of the Caribbean as it turns almost green over the coral reefs of Isla Mujeres. *One minus one does not equal zero*, I tell myself. *It equals one.*

COLLATERAL DAMAGE

WE WERE BOUNCING along a dirt road in Ernie's pickup, sticks of dynamite between us on the bench seat like sausages packed in green casings. I was sitting on the passenger's side, cradling the detonator caps between my legs. Old Ernie must have seen something in my eyes every time he hit a pothole. "You sufferin' from a nervous debility or somethin'?" he asked.

That dynamite was leaping in the air like it had a mind of its own every time Ernie hit a bump in the road. "Just wondering," I yelled to Ernie over the noise of his V8 oil-burner, "when one of those sticks of dynamite might go off."

Everything I needed to know by the age of fifteen, I had learned from our neighbour Ernie. He was an old-time handyman, equally at home punching a well or castrating a pig. Ernie never went to school for anything; he just learned by doing. He'd blown himself up once or twice in the process of acquiring an education, as you could tell by observing that he only had three fingers on his left hand. He'd been a freight hopper during the Depression when work was scarce. He told me stories of sleeping on top of boxcars as they were careening through the Rocky

Mountains, of climbing to the tops of Douglas firs when he was able to get a job as a lumberjack, of seeing the Pacific Ocean for the first time. I had never seen the ocean. Being around Ernie was one wall-to-wall adventure; you didn't know what was going to happen next.

Ernie never said why he used to call on me to help out with his adventures, but I think he liked me because I was a handy kid. I'd taken it upon myself to do a ring-and-valve job on my dad's old Massey-Harris the winter I turned twelve. When my dad told him about my foray into motor mechanics, I could see Ernie's eyes light up. I think Ernie decided that I was a likely recipient for all the knowledge he had so painfully gained, and so he frequently invited me to join him on his excursions to the hinterlands to build barbwire fences or punch a well. My dad must have trusted Ernie at least a little bit because he gave me permission to go on those jaunts whenever he had no need of me on the farm.

Still, given Ernie's lack of any kind of formal training and the fact that I had never before accompanied him on a quest involving the use of explosives, I think I had every right to be nervous about that dynamite. Ernie let out that wheezy, snotty laugh of his, the kind of laugh you could easily mistake for a fit of emphysema, and he called out merrily, "Hell, kid, it ain't the dynamite ya gotta worry about. It's them detonator caps you got pressed against your left nut that'll kill ya."

IT'S that attitude of "don't think about it, just do it" that got me where I am today. Which is sitting in the Hooters in the West Edmonton Mall on a blustery autumn day with two besuited Department of National Defence officials and an Air Force officer in full military regalia. The National Defence guys wanted to set up the meeting off-campus somewhere, away from the constraints of academe. I guess Hooters is about as far from academe as you can get.

The Air Force officer does all the talking. "We're here to discuss your research, Dr. Fitzgerald."

My research could be a lot of things. As part of the university's aeronautical team, I've helped send Swedish satellites into space. God knows what payloads were on them. I've done research on the electromagnetic charge of the aurora borealis. I've worked with NASA on flight trajectories and gravitational pull. "What research are you talking about?"

The officer looks at the National Defence officials. "These guys didn't tell you why we wanted to set up a meeting?"

"They just told me to be here."

"That's standard procedure," mutters one of the defence guys, the older, chunkier one.

Just then, the waitress appears at our table. She's wearing the traditional Hooters costume and the traditional *I know you can't keep your eyes off my breasts* smile. "Gentlemen," she says. "Coffee to start with?"

All three of my compatriots glue their eyes to the table. They are at work, and they can't be seen to let their judgment be clouded by the sight of surgically augmented boobs.

When the waitress has taken her mini-skirted butt back to the kitchen, our conversation continues. "We understand," says the Air Force guy, "you've been working on an articulated wing."

This has been a side project, really: an articulated wing, much like a sparrow's, that might allow an airplane to land in tight places. I was thinking of bush pilots in the Canadian north, guys who have to land on rivers between two rock ledges. I got the idea while watching my kid try to land his model airplane in our tiny backyard near the Mill Creek Ravine. "I haven't worked all the bugs out yet," I tell the Air Force guy.

The three of them glance at one another again. Then the Air

Force guy says, "We think this could have a practical application for the military."

"Oh?" I say. "In what way?"

The Air Force guy smiles benevolently. "You should let us worry about that," he says. "Would you be willing to sell your patent to the Government of Canada?"

There's plenty about this I don't like, all this cloak-and-dagger government stuff. I didn't get a PhD in engineering so that I could manufacture weapons of mass destruction. "The university owns the patents on all my research."

One of the government guys, the younger one, speaks up. "Of course, we'll talk to the university about this, but we wanted to get your blessing first."

"I'll have to think about it."

The pretty waitress returns to our table with a notepad in hand. "Are we ready to order, gentlemen?"

"We'll make it worth your while," the older government guy says under his breath while his colleague orders a meal.

"I'll have to think about it."

BECAUSE IT WAS EARLY in the spring, snow lay in uneven furrows across the fields. Ernie piloted his truck as close to the creek as he could get. The elderly half-ton shuddered like a dying horse as Ernie brought it to a stop. I was glad the bumpy ride had ended.

Ernie grabbed the box of dynamite and climbed gingerly out of the truck. He always moved kind of gingerly because of all his injuries. He told me that he'd broken his back once when he was run over by the packers on his daddy's farm. He had a bent-over Walter Brennan hunch when he walked and the limp to go along with it. "Bring them detonators," he wheezed, "and not in yer back pocket, either. And bring that wrecking bar out of the box." I clutched a handful of detonator caps delicately in the palm of my hand, retrieved the wrecking bar, and followed him across the field toward the creek.

We picked our way along the creek bed up to where the beaver dam interfered with the current of cold, dark water. It wasn't a huge dam—it didn't have to be to stop up a creek that size. There was a stick-and-mud lodge just upstream of the dam. If people built their houses as sturdily as that beaver built her lodge, those houses would last a hundred years.

Ernie spat a wad of green phlegm onto the snow. "We're gonna have to blow the lodge, too," he said. "Otherwise, she'll just build up that dam again."

It was the first time I thought that maybe we would be out there killing beavers. I don't know why I hadn't thought of it before. When Ernie asked me to come along with him, I thought we were going to have a merry time getting the creek to run again. No animals would need to be harmed in the course of our adventure.

We started with the dam first. Ernie did some vague calisthenics to limber up his arthritic shoulders, and then he showed me how to tamp holes in the frozen mud. It was hard work because the permafrost was still in the ground, and the holes had to be two feet deep.

While I thrust the wrecking bar mindlessly into the top of the dam, Ernie was busy crimping the detonator caps between his teeth and inserting the business end of the caps into the sticks of dynamite. He connected all of the caps with a common fuse, which he'd measured out at two arm's lengths. When I was finished with the tamping, Ernie slid a stick of dynamite down each hole. He had to be careful not to disturb the detonator caps or the fuse. I backed off a little way. "Aren't you worried they'll go off?" I asked.

"It's the ones that don't go off ya gotta worry about," he growled. "Cuz then you have to come back in here and dig 'em up again."

At last, the dynamite was set, and Ernie was poised next to the fuse with a Bic lighter in hand. "We'll walk that way out into the field," he said. "If you wanna head start, you better get goin' now."

I wanted to show Ernie that I was brave, that I was the same kind of badass guy who might have ridden the rails with him in 1935. "I'll wait and walk with you."

He lit the fuse and made sure it was going well. "Let's walk," he said.

Ernie walked as briskly as an old man who had once broken his back could, and that was none too briskly. I matched him step for step, silent at first, but when we were a good thirty yards away, I asked him, "How do you know how much fuse to set?"

He looked at me with a wry smile. "I just guesstimate," he said, "like I do with everythin' else in life."

We waited for what seemed like a long time out there on the cold prairie. The wind was starting to pick up, and I was wishing I had worn my winter parka and not just an old baseball jacket. "Shit!" Ernie said, finally. "Piss-eyed fuse musta gone out." I was alert to the anxiety in his voice, a tone I'd never heard from him before. "You stay here."

"I'm comin' with you, Ernie."

"I told you to stay here," he wheezed as we headed back toward the dam. "Yer old man would never forgive me if . . ." He managed to say that many words before I heard the explosion. And then I saw a cloud of mud, water, and lumber descending upon us like the wrath of God, and that was the last I saw before I was airborne, too.

"THIS IS REALLY GOING to put us on the map," George says. "I can't tell you how momentous this is." George is our department head. It's three weeks before the Christmas break, and we're sitting in his unctuous office, all leather furniture bought cut-rate at some wholesale warehouse in the city. The university's serviceable desks and chairs were not good enough for George.

"It's difficult for me to get too excited about this," I say. "It's not even the main thrust of my research. Stephen and I just got talking about it one day, and the next thing I knew, it was happening." I'm sunk three feet deep into George's leather couch; I always feel like I'm slightly helpless when I enter this room, like I'm caught in a quicksand of leather. It would take six horses and a stick of dynamite to hoist me out of this couch.

George offers me his most winning smile. He should have been a television news announcer, with his slicked-back hair and perfect teeth. "Sometimes the most momentous research is also the most serendipitous," he purrs. "Look at Banting and penicillin."

The word *serendipitous* sticks in my craw. You might think you're growing cultures in petri dishes, but you're really curing diseases. You might think of a hundred and one uses for your research, but there's always someone who can think of one more. "Yes, but I don't like it," I tell George, "trafficking with the military."

George leans back in his leather chair. "We all know how the sausage is made, Merv," he says. "Countries go to war sometimes with little reason, but that doesn't mean we shouldn't support the war effort. That doesn't mean we shouldn't do our patriotic duty."

Patriotic duty be damned. I didn't spend my formative years in the '60s without a little indoctrination into the anti-war protests of that time. "I'm not in this business to kill people."

"At least, then," George says, leaning forward and toying with a fountain pen on his leather desk mat, "at least, then, think of your colleagues and the wellbeing of the department. Stephen was the second author on your paper. How much work did he put into it?"

"His work on the project was minimal," I say. "He looked at some of the wind tunnel data. That was all."

"Still," says George, "I would imagine that Stephen wouldn't mind having National Defence funding at this early stage in his career. If we land this contract with the military, good things will follow. Grants. Graduate students. More faculty positions."

"That's all fanfare and public relations bullshit," I say. "I've been doing quality research all along, and nobody's taken much notice. Now, suddenly, the military wants in, and we get more faculty positions?"

"We all know how the sausage is made," George repeats. "Not to mention the publicity you'll get for yourself. I can see you getting your picture on the cover of *Maclean's*."

You've got to hand it to George. He really loves all this public relations stuff; it's not just a hobby for him. "I'm not a politician," I tell him.

George straightens his tie. "Well, at least think about it," he says. "In the meantime, I've gotten in touch with the university president about this matter. He's extremely excited to see it go ahead."

I manage to hoist myself out of George's sofa. "I wish you wouldn't have done that, George."

"This is a big deal, Merv," he says. "I'm not sure you realize how big of a deal it is."

ON THAT COLD PRAIRIE DAY, I arrived at an understanding of what it might be like to be in the middle of a bomb blast.

You're disoriented. You feel light in the head. And the world around you has turned topsy-turvy.

I sat up in the dirt field. Ernie was standing above me, looking slightly crazed, a gash on his ancient forehead where he must have been whacked with flying debris. He spat another wad of phlegm on the ground. "Looks like I miscalculated on the length of the fuse," he said. "You okay, kid?"

"Yeah."

"It's all clear now," he wheezed. "Listen to the sound of that babbling brook. We blew that dam good!"

We started back toward the site of the explosion. The creek bed below the dam was nearly overflowing with water. All was right with the world. At the time, I thought that Ernie and I had helped Mother Nature do her work. The remnants of well-chewed poplar were strewn across the landscape.

"Yesirree," Ernie said, "we blew that dam good!" He performed a little Walter Brennan jig right there beside the creek.

The next order of business was to take care of the lodge. Ernie set me up tamping the holes again while he prepared the dynamite. I asked him if he thought we were going to be killing any beavers.

"Hell, no, kid," he said, the butt of a cigarette smouldering in his mouth. "If she knows what's good for her, that beaver is six miles upstream by now."

The dome of that lodge was so thick with mud and wood that I couldn't tell if there was a living space inside. It had been built to withstand all sorts of natural disasters, everything from floods to frost to snowstorms. We set six charges at intervals deep in the walls of the lodge. Ernie measured out two arm's lengths of fuse. Bending down gingerly, he touched his lit cigarette to the fuse's end.

We walked away briskly.

The explosion was spectacular from our vantage point in a

bluff of trees fifty yards away. It seemed as though some unseen hand had lifted the beaver lodge twenty feet in the air, and then the lodge vaporized in a haze of mud, water, and wood.

I'M FLYING into Ottawa with the university's vice president of research, Jacinder Singh, a week later. I don't usually fly first class, but this ticket is paid for by the Government of Canada. It's easy to fall into that first-class smugness as you're sitting there with your glass of wine in a seat that you wish you had in your own living room, watching the plebes shuffle through with their two pieces of hand baggage and twenty-pound babies attached to their hips.

Vice President Singh sits beside me during the flight. He's a sharp fellow, but he deports himself like an everyman. He's never seen in a suit, and he loves to talk about Indian cricket. "The best cricket in the world," he says, "because they play the year round." I know nothing about the sport.

Two government guys meet us at the airport and drive us into town in their nondescript Toyota. They're a little more upscale than the guys I met in Edmonton. Their suits are a little costlier. They have more expensive haircuts.

We end up in a downtown boardroom. Two more men are waiting for me, and they look like they've been waiting a long time, like maybe their entire life consists of sitting in rooms and waiting for people. They stand up when I'm escorted into the room, and the first guy introduces himself as an executive assistant in the Department of National Defence. The guy looks to be about twenty-five years old, one of those nerds I've seen on campus who spends his time running for student council. He's bright, though, and charming as a trained seal.

"I'd like you to meet Mike Cavillo," he says, gesturing

toward the guy beside him. "Mike is the assistant deputy minister in charge of military research and innovation here in Ottawa."

I give the fellow the once-over as I'm shaking his hand. He's middle-aged, with Coke-bottle spectacles and a tweed blazer. He might easily be mistaken for the manager of your local bank.

"I'm very pleased to meet you, Professor Fitzgerald." He speaks in the slow, measured cadence of a government official. "You're the man of the hour."

"Hopefully not the eleventh hour," I say. Either no one gets the joke, or no one wants to share in my black humour.

We all sit down at one end of a massive boardroom table. "So," the kid from the Department of Defence begins, "the articulated wing. We read your article in the *Journal of Impact Engineering* with great interest."

"I'm surprised," I admit, "that you guys have time to read journal articles."

"When they're about articulated wings," Cavillo interjects, "we read 'em."

"We understand that you have a patent on your research," the kid continues. "We'll cut to the chase. We're offering three point five million dollars for the exclusive right to bring your research to fruition." This takes my breath away. "Is that not enough?" the kid asks.

"Three point five million is lots," I say. "Maybe too much."

Vice President Singh enters the conversation. "Professor Fitzgerald's research has the potential to be far-reaching in the aviation industry," he says. "It might be used in all sorts of scenarios. We would expect an investment of at least ten million for rights to use the patent."

Cavillo and the kid look at each other. "Ten million dollars," Cavillo says, and he whistles softly to himself.

The kid nods his head.

"Then ten million dollars it is," Cavillo says, looking back at us. "Do we have a deal?"

I can tell Jacinder had expected an old-fashioned bartering. He looks slightly shaken, but he says, "Yes, we have a deal."

"That's good, then," Cavillo says. "Let's draw up the contract."

"I just don't know if I want to do this," I say quickly.

There's a hush in the room, as though all those oak walls and high-backed chairs have swallowed up the sound. Jacinder Singh looks at me as if I've lost my mind. "We're offering you ten million dollars," the government kid repeats. "That's a lot of money for what you do."

"Maybe so," I reply. "I just don't know that I want to kill people for that price."

Cavillo smiles at me beneficently. "Don't think of it as killing people," he says. "Think of it as saving lives back here in good old North America."

The kid looks down at the shiny tabletop for a long time. "Have you talked to your university president about this?"

Jacinder speaks up again. "We've had a word with him, yes."

"This deal could do a lot for the reputation of your university." The kid is pretty steely all of a sudden like he wants to play hardball with me.

"I'm sure it could," I reply, "but I'm going to need some time to think about this."

"I wouldn't take too long," Cavillo says, grinning. "The Americans, down in Bethesda, are working on a project very similar to yours, even as we speak. Your Canadian patent won't mean a goddamn thing to them down there."

"They can do what they want," I reply.

"If I were you," he says, "I'd take the money while I can get it."

"Is this meeting over?" I ask the kid.

"Just one more thing," the kid says. "I understand Professor Stephen Thorenson is the second author on your article?"

"That's right."

"Professor Thorenson," he says, "landed a small grant from National Defence three years ago."

He knows he has me, the little bastard. "That was for his work on minesweepers," I tell the kid. "Not for this project."

The kid pulls a piece of paper out of his briefcase. "The contract reads that the department is entitled to use the products of his research in any way it sees fit. And that, according to my reading, includes any and all research he is involved in at your university, with or without further remuneration."

WHEN WE ARRIVED at the rise where the lodge had been, I saw insanity in the dark water. Something was darting around down there, in tight circles, a foot below the water's surface. There was something in my fifteen-year-old self that didn't want to look, that didn't want to know the madness we had wrought. But there was also something that drew me in with hypnotic suggestion, that wouldn't let me look away.

Two kits were dead in the water, bobbing up and down like furry children's toys that had been left in the swimming pool overnight. Their mother was the creature I had glimpsed still moving beneath the water's surface. She swam effortlessly in her endless circles, her paws and tail moving in tandem as though nothing were out of the ordinary. As though this happened every day. When I got closer, I could see that she was swimming on her back. Her world had gone topsy-turvy. The creek bed was the roof over her head, and the lowering sky was the hole she had fallen through to another dimension.

Ernie saw the horror on my face, and he told me to look away.

He picked up the wrecking bar and began thrashing the water with it. The beaver had lost her equilibrium. She didn't know how to dive and elude the manic attack of the wrecking bar. Even in her vulnerable position, it took her a long time to die.

We rode silently back to my father's farmyard that chilly afternoon. As I was getting out of the truck, Ernie looked at me and said, "Collateral damage, kid. Don't let it bother ya." It did, though, and I never worked another job with Ernie after that.

"IT'S A RED-LETTER DAY," my wife tells me, adjusting my tie in the front room of our Mill Creek home. We're getting ready for a graduation ceremony on a bright morning in May. A cup of coffee stands, half-empty, on my bookshelf. I'm never happy in a suit. I feel like a child going unwillingly to a choir practice. "The Distinguished Researcher Award," my wife says. "That's something to be proud of."

I look at myself in the mirror above the piano. What stares back at me is someone with a hangdog look. "I'm not so certain."

"You should be thrilled," my wife says. "Your research is celebrated the world over. You've landed a National Defence contract for the university, and they've used that money to build a new lab in your name." She pats me on the shoulder to let me know that I'm fit for public consumption. "You look gorgeous."

"No," I say, "you look gorgeous. I look like Will Geer on a bad day."

IT'S FIVE YEARS LATER, and I'm newly retired now, sitting in front of the television in our living room. The news anchor is telling us about all the wildfires burning across northern Alberta.

After a brief segue, he launches into a description of a military manoeuvre gone wrong. As he continues with his report, military footage is shown of a drone flying into a city centre somewhere in Asia. The ancient buildings are three and four stories high in every direction. If you look closely, you can see that as the drone veers into an alley, its wings fold like a sparrow's. There is a moment of nothingness, then a detonation flash from an open window at the end of the alley, and then a large building disintegrates. There is no sign of the people inside.

After the blast is shown from two different angles, the announcer describes the carnage. "A Canadian-made drone," he intones, "was guided accidentally into a garment factory in Pakistan today. The death toll has not been verified, but reports suggest that at least fifty-eight women and children were killed in the explosion." They cut to a military analyst who calls the accident and the resulting deaths "collateral damage that was unavoidable, given the circumstances."

My wife scurries to find the remote. She switches off the television. "You're not responsible," she says.

"I made that possible." I have no more words. I'm not normally a crier, but tears are running down my face. I gesture vaguely toward the blank TV screen. It's all too much.

My wife looks at me the way women look at men when they want to help but can't. "No," she says as matter-of-factly as she can, "other people made that possible."

I'd like to believe her, but all I can think about is old Ernie thrashing at that goddamned beaver with his wrecking bar.

HOW TO BE HAPPY

PROFESSOR AL BRACKEN knew something was wrong when his inscrutable oracle of a department head, Doctor Noushad Ananthakrishnan, invited him in to discuss his teaching evaluations. Noush always started with a compliment. "My very, very esteemed colleague, Doctor Bracken!" he exclaimed. "Come in! Come in!" A good fifteen minutes after Al had sat down on the ornate chair opposite the department head's desk, Noush finally got to the point. "We must discuss, my most learned friend, we must discuss the teaching evaluations. This is a matter of procedure, something I must do every year with every faculty member. But we must discuss."

Al had seen the evaluations, and they weren't good. "The students hate me," he said. "They hate me because I don't hand out nineties for bullshit like Martin does."

Noush sat up straight in his chair and looked at Al inscrutably. He was perhaps organizing his thoughts. Or maybe not. "Fair enough, fair enough," he said at last, bobbling his head from side to side. "But some of these evaluations are even more scathing than in past years."

He handed a piece of wrinkled paper to Al. An anonymous student's evaluative statement was scribbled on it in lettering of which a four-year-old might have been proud. Al managed to decipher the last sentence despite the calligraphy. "A monkey could have taught this class better."

Al smiled inwardly, recalling the string bean kid at the back of one of his Western Religions classes. The kid did have some spunk in him after all, even if he had spent his time Googling Saturday Night Live sketches on his cell phone during Al's lectures. "Are you gonna believe someone who's still writing at a Grade 3 level?" he asked Noush.

"I do not know what to believe, my honoured friend," Noush replied, looking over the top of his spectacles. "But if these reviews continue into next year, we will have to talk about remedial measures."

Just what remedial measures Noush was going on about, Al had no idea. The Religious Studies department was understaffed at the best of times; Noush couldn't be contemplating relieving him of his teaching assignment. Maybe remedial measures meant that Al would teach more classes rather than fewer. What he had pitifully called his research program had fallen off in recent years. He was no longer considered worthy of an SSHRC grant, the litmus test these days of whether a faculty member was ultimately valued. And his publications record was paltry, to the point where the previous year's output had been a book review in *Pastoral Psychology*.

Al momentarily regretted the fact that he lectured from the same notes he'd started teaching with in 1978, notes that were gleaned from his own freshman religious studies course with old Doctor McCrimmon, he of the incorrigible mumble and the Tullamore Dew on his breath. Al vaguely remembered being a well-regarded teacher in his younger years, probably owing to the proximity of his own age to the ages of the students back then.

They had figured he was cool with his hippie ponytail and his unorthodox views. Now, with his ponytail gone and his unorthodox views held by almost everyone, he was deemed a mediocre teacher.

IT ALL CAME to a head after the mid-term break in February. Instead of going south for a vacation as he should have done, Al spent the week ensconced in his four-foot-by-eight-foot den in his bungalow on Fourteenth Street, marking exams. He found himself writing bold statements in the margins of the exam papers, things like, "Your syntactical infelicities have made a drone strike on my will to live" and "Your non-argumentative tone has done a Vulcan mind-meld number on me." He had wielded his red pen like a berserker's axe all week long, and when it came time to hand the papers back to the students on the following Monday, he was tired and fuming at the injustice of having to grade substandard exams while his sun-kissed students had jetted off to Mexico with their well-heeled parents. The highest mark he gave on the exam was a saucy fifty-nine to a student who had half a brain and half an understanding of the art of disputation but could have done better.

On that blustery February Monday, while the snow fell like caked cow dung from a grey sky, Al stumbled into the classroom and handed out pamphlets and application forms to the twenty-one students who were in attendance. The application forms were for postings at McDonalds and Costco. "Before we do anything today," Al announced, "I want you to fill out these application forms. Judging by the quality of the examination papers I received, these are the only jobs of which you will be capable in two years' time." He then yanked the marked examination papers from his briefcase and flung them in the air, watching as they wafted to the floor by the podium like paratroopers storming enemy lines. There was a solemn moment when Al stared red-eyed at the stupid herd of students in front of him and when they stared blank-faced back. "Read Chapter 7 of Theodore's *Sacred Paths* for Wednesday," he said through gritted teeth. "It contains the secret of life." Then, with a derisive exhalation, Al marched out of the classroom.

Of course, there were more meetings with Noush after that and even a visit from the Faculty Help Office. The woman from Faculty Help sat opposite Al in his cubicle in the Arts Building, placed her bejewelled hand on his elbow, and asked if he was considering a temporary leave of absence.

"There's nothing wrong with me," Al retorted.

"Are you happy here?"

"Why should I be?"

"Everybody deserves to be happy," said the woman.

"Everybody deserves to pursue happiness," Al corrected her. "Whether they get it or not is another thing."

By that time, Al had pretty much given up on the pursuit of happiness. He had believed all the bullshit they told him in his younger years, how by dint of hard work and accomplishment, you could have it all—the car, the house, the Stanley Cup wife. Through his years of graduate school and his early life as a professor, he had never been able to afford more than a Honda Civic and a Nutana bungalow. As for the trophy wife, his genetics had gotten in the way. All of his forefathers were five foot three with heads like ten-pin bowling balls, including the holes, and so was Al. Not exactly an industrial-strength electromagnet for chicks. Oh, sure, he'd had it off with the odd graduate student over the years, but they had pretty much made it clear, when they went to bed with him, that they were looking for a good letter of reference or perhaps a sessional posting in the department.

After promising Noush that he would at least try to be good

over the remaining six weeks of term, Al managed to keep all of his classes. The students, however, had declared all-out war on him, wasting their time and his by peppering him with inane questions in class and coming in large groups to his office to argue about term papers.

On top of all of this, Al was enlisted against his will to serve on the department's hiring committee. With the imminent retirement of their academic star, John Martin, the committee was given the green light to hire a replacement in Oriental Religions. They'd narrowed the search down to three candidates: a professor from a university in Agra who was aching to emigrate to North America, even to a frozen wasteland on the Canadian prairies; a hot-shot young PhD from Indiana; and a Taoist monk from Shandong who happened to be visiting friends in Toronto. The committee's initial interviews were to be conducted via Zoom, although Al spoke against it. The Luddite in him didn't trust infernal machines, and he argued that much was lost in the translation. Body language was important, he said; without seeing the candidates face-to-face, you couldn't tell if they were stroking your ego or slipping you the finger out of frame.

On a Monday morning in early March, the committee gathered in the departmental seminar room for the Zoom sessions. They met at 8:30, not Al's favourite hour since he'd been suffering from insomnia these last years. But 8:30 a.m. in Saskatoon was 8 p.m. in Agra, so accommodations had to be made.

The candidate from Agra, one Doctor Mohammed Bihkshu, had set himself up in a booth at an internet café somewhere in the city's centre. The internet signal was, as Al predicted, extremely weak, and the image, which was projected on the large screen at one end of the seminar room, frequently chunked up and sometimes was lost altogether. Still, you could hear the roadrunner horns of auto rickshaws and the sounds of humanity, elephants, and God-knew-what-else out in the street. You could practically smell the chai and the curry, and Al felt a twinge of longing for those days when he used to travel, when he was engaged in active research.

The committee asked a pre-screened set of questions. "Why have you applied for this job?" "Tell us about your teaching philosophy." "Once hired at this university, what would your research goals be?"

The candidate responded as best he could. Because his English was weak—a fact unbeknownst to the committee when they shortlisted him—and because he knew that Noush was a fellow Indian, the candidate occasionally lapsed into Hindi, which left Al and his colleague John Martin out in the cold. To top it off, the camera in that internet booth in Agra was placed at such an awkward angle that the hiring committee spent most of the interview looking directly up Mohammed Bihkshu's left nostril.

"Tell us about your area of expertise," Al shouted at the video screen, as though shouting would make his statement more comprehensible to the candidate.

There was the usual five-second delay while Al's verbalization bounced from satellite to satellite. "I beg your pardon, sir?" the candidate replied, equally as loud.

"Your. Area. Of. Expertise," Al yelled. "What. Is. It?"

"Eeria of hexpertise?"

"Yes!"

"Ees the five paths of Chinese religiouse thought. The paths of accumulation, of joining, of seeing, of meditation. And the path of no more learning."

After the interview was over and the candidate had signed off, Noush was complimentary. He had clearly gleaned more from the conversation than his colleagues. "Well, my honoured friends," he said, "Mohammed Bihkshu clearly knows his subject area."

Al glanced sidelong at John Martin. "I suppose," Al said, "if you could only understand what the man was saying."

Noush looked shocked. "I understood him very well."

Good Saint John Martin had to agree with Al for once, and when John Martin spoke, he spoke with the voice of rationality. "We cannot subject our students," he intoned, "to a professor who can't make himself understood."

"Very well, very well," Noush said with a side-to-side head bobble. "We will go on to our next candidate."

The next candidate was Doctor Aleisha Doherty, newly graduated from the University of Indiana. She was about twenty-seven years old, according to her CV, and her CV was impressive. Doctor Doherty was haughty and beautiful—perhaps too haughty, Al thought, even given her extensive resume. She stood ramrod straight and did not suffer fools gladly. Al hated her almost instantly as her unblemished face appeared on the projection screen. This was the young woman, right here, who served as a prototype for all those others who had rejected Al with a derisive smile and a merry walk-away. This was the prototype for all those young women who had sat on Al's ratty sofa and explained to him that there was simply no attraction. Al watched her interview and grew progressively glummer with each word she said. He asked her a question about the title of her PhD dissertation, and she replied curtly, "Why? Does the title bother you?"

When the interview was over, Al could tell that John Martin was smitten with her. "She's quite talented," John Martin said quietly, thus crowning her the leader of the foot race.

The final candidate that morning was Doctor Soo Xiaping, the Taoist monk, whose image was Zoomed from a laptop in the living room of his friend's spare apartment in Toronto. Xiaping was a young man, maybe thirty-five, affable as hell, his head shaved clean in the usual manner of men of his order. The smile never left his face. It seemed to Al that the man had discarded his woes with his hair. "If you are invited for an in-person interview here," Al asked him, "what will the title of your presentation be?"

The young Taoist had an accent, but it was not insurmountable. "I think I shall speak about happiness," he said, "and how best to attain it."

Al was skeptical about the proposed presentation topic, but he also knew that he had a thing or two to learn about happiness. What was there to lose? The Dean's Office had given them the green light to fly in two candidates, and Al would see himself in hell before he would countenance an interview with the unintelligible professor from Agra

In the end, the committee decided to invite the fetching Ms. Doherty and the cheery Mr. Xiaping for face-to-face interviews.

IN EARLY APRIL, when classes ended, Al's students marched *en masse* to Noush's office and demanded that Al be fired. They showed Noush the angry comments Al had scribbled on their midterm exams and argued that Al was customarily rude and insulting. His lectures were boring, they said, because he simply stood at the front of the classroom and read from his musty, yellowing notes. Sometimes, he didn't bother to make eye contact with his students for an entire fifty-minute class; he just buried his face in his lecture notes, only glancing up now and then to see what was going on outside his classroom window. On those occasions, he would stare catatonically as if Martians were landing in the green space between the Arts Tower and Law. It was as if the lecture had gone into a time warp, they told Noush, until Al would remember himself and resume speaking in mid-sentence. Worst of all, said a blonde girl, he leered at the women. "He never looks me in the eyes when he talks to me," she said, her own eyes deep with meaning.

Noush could see why Al didn't look her in the eyes. "Yes, thank you all, thank you very much," he said to the students as they were filing out of his office. "You may rest assured in your deep heart's core that I will have this dealt with most summarily. Most summarily."

After the students had left his office, Noush thought about the difficult conversation he would need to have with Professor Bracken. And then Noush did what he often did; he decided to put off that conversation to a much later date.

THE CANDIDATES for the Oriental Religions position arrived two weeks later. The first of these, Doctor Doherty from the University of Indiana, landed in Saskatoon early on Monday morning. John Martin had agreed to pick her up at the airport, and by the time they arrived at the university for her presentation to the faculty, Martin and she were getting along like Henry Miller and Anais Nin. She laughed at all of Martin's milquetoast jokes, and Al noticed that she kept a lingering hand on the well-worn elbow of Martin's corduroy blazer for longer than was required.

Her presentation was a travelogue, basically, of her latest trip to China and all the temples and tourist sites she'd visited there. In her PowerPoint, she flashed a fine set of teeth at the camera as several Chinese academics jockeyed for position beside her. At the Tianning Temple, she gazed appreciatively upon the shrine as a collection of tourists and locals gazed appreciatively upon her voluptuousness. "I really didn't get much from your presentation," Al said in his usual confrontational fashion. "Can you tell us anything that we don't know about Buddhist thought?"

"I wouldn't presume to teach this group anything that it doesn't already know," Ms. Doherty demurred, "but I can assure you that I am a fount of knowledge on Oriental religions and a darn good teacher."

She did, in fact, teach well later that afternoon with a cadre of handpicked upper-year students who had agreed to volunteer some of their study time for the betterment of the department. She taught a module on "Spiritual Love in the Buddhist Tradition," at one point draping her long legs over the desk at the front of the classroom and announcing that Buddhism placed fewer restraints upon sexual love than, say, Christianity. The young men in the classroom were particularly appreciative.

The exit interview was a love-in. Al felt out of place in that territory. He incurred the wrath of his colleagues by asking the young woman if she had a husband or a boyfriend who might also be looking to immigrate to Canada. Before she could answer, John Martin interceded, declaring that Al's question was in violation of the human rights code. "The candidate's personal life is her personal business," he barked authoritatively.

Al shook his head. "I'm only wondering," he said, "what's to prevent the candidate from arriving here and getting pregnant immediately, thus keeping a short-staffed department continually short-staffed for an indefinite number of years?"

The candidate gasped, John Martin was red-faced, and Noush knew it was time to intervene. "I must really put an end to the interview now, my dear, dear friends," he said evenly. "We are past the hour, and our reservation for dinner is waiting on us."

TWO DAYS LATER, Soo Xiaping blew into town like a fresh sea wind. He was even more ebullient in person than he had been in the chunked-up pseudo-reality of Zoom. He walked with the easy gait of a man who had embraced the animal within. He was devoid of pretension. Al perched on a chair in the seminar room, watching the young man prepare a media cart for his presentation. "I am not good with technology," Xiaping admitted, smiling broadly at the assembled hiring committee. Almost against his will, Al found himself smiling back.

When the presentation was ready to begin, and when the committee had topped up their stained mugs with strong black coffee, Xiaping flicked the light switch at the back of the room and started the DVD player by remote. The legend "How To Be Happy" appeared on the projection screen, followed by a scene from a computer-animated movie called *Kung Fu Panda*. In the scene, an overweight panda bear proved himself worthy of the dragon scroll, a scroll purported to have written on it the secret of life, located high in the cartoon rafters. After a series of acrobatic kung fu moves, the panda bear's master procured the scroll by balancing a flower petal on one end of it. The bear examined the scroll in the manner of one who cannot figure out how to open a jar of pickles because the lid is too tight. At last, his master opened the scroll for him, and the panda unfurled it. Shock registered on the bear's face. "What is written there?" his master wanted to know.

"Nothing."

"Nothing?"

"Nothing."

Al turned to John Martin and whispered, "Well, I'm happy already."

At the conclusion of the video clip, Xiaping turned the lights back on and strolled to the front of the room. He seemed too completely at ease for somebody who was vying for a coveted university teaching job. "How to be happy," he began. "There is no tomorrow and no yesterday. There is only this present moment. But for what you do, the arrow will find its bullseye."

Al resisted Xiaping's message at first. He didn't like all that Zen bullshit about shooting arrows without really caring where they landed. He sat and smiled and watched and learned, and gradually, almost by hypnotic suggestion, he gained an appreciation of Xiaping's way of seeing.

It was a sea change. Al was like a boat gently tossing to and fro in the heart of a becalmed ocean. He found himself looking at his own life *sub specie aeternitatis*. Here he was, possibly five years from retirement, with no joy in the present moment. He had been consumed by tomorrows and yesterdays throughout his career. A sea change was needed.

AFTER XIAPING HAD DEPARTED for Toronto, the committee met one last time to make the hire. Al spoke in favour of Xiaping but found himself up against a barrage of arguments from his colleagues. Xiaping had been too esoteric, they said. His credentials were in question, coming from a religious institution in China nobody had ever heard of. He was perhaps too laid back for a department bent on improving its record in procuring research grants.

Al's initial impulse was to debate with vehemence, but he found himself thinking that nothing would be resolved through acrimony. He listened without a *soupçon* of ego as his colleagues made their arguments. *If they could only see themselves*, he thought as he watched their lips move, *they would recognize their own smallness.* They had set themselves apart from nature and had shown neither humility nor grace. They had lost their sense of *wu-wei.*

In the end, they voted to hire the haughty woman from Indiana. Well, Al thought, perhaps he was being a little unfair. She was a pretty good teacher.

OVER THE SUMMER, Al devised a new syllabus for the one class Noush was prepared to let him teach. It was a freshman course entitled "World Religions," which would be taught to 150 fresh-faced high school graduates. Perhaps Noush thought that freshmen would be less likely to complain than more savvy upper-year students.

Al found himself rereading the *Tao Te Ching* of Laozi with a renewed sense of excitement. He planned to introduce a two-week segment on Taoism into the course, although he was by no means an expert on that particular tradition. He tweaked his syllabus almost daily, right up to the first day of classes.

While walking in the park in August, Al noticed a group of Chinese martial arts enthusiasts working through a *kata* in slow motion. He stopped and watched for a few minutes, and during a break in the action, he asked one of them what they were doing. "*Tai chi,*" a young man said. "Would you care to join?"

"Possibly," he heard himself say.

"Feel free."

Al hadn't done anything impulsive in years, and he was hesitant to join in at a moment's notice. "I'll have to think about it. Are you back here next weekend?"

"Rain or shine."

Al was no martial artist, and he wasn't looking to develop new skills so late in life. He went home and put a TV dinner into the microwave.

That night, he had difficulty sleeping. Xiaping's words resonated in his head. *There is no tomorrow and no yesterday. There is only the present moment.*

A week later, Al found himself walking in the same park. The young man he had spoken to earlier greeted Al and encouraged him to join. It didn't matter that he was in his street clothes. It didn't matter that the grass was wet.

Al kicked off his shoes and adopted the initial pose of the

kata. As he followed the leader through a series of manoeuvres, he got lost in the physical changes that were taking place inside his own body. The city melted away behind him, and he was standing in a green park surrounded by nothingness. His body melted away from him, too, and he was all spirit, one with the rest of his brethren, one with the irrepressible rhythms of the earth.

WHEN AL WALKED into the classroom that autumn, he was ten pounds lighter, both physically and mentally. The *tai chi* had done its work. He looked into the expectant faces of the teenagers who were chattering in the lecture hall, and then he strolled over to the media consul and pressed a button. The Kung Fu Panda performed a series of *kung fu* moves on the screen at the front of the classroom. When the video presentation had finished, Al waded into the no-man's land between the blackboard and the students. He told them about the hunchback on the Silk Road. "If my hand was an axe," he said, "I would chop wood. If my hand was a rooster, I would crow at the break of day."

Al looked into the eyes of his students, and it dawned on him that they were on the edge of their seats, as caught up in the moment as he. None of them were checking their phones for the latest Facebook post. One kid, a gangly youth with an Iroquois haircut, placed his pen neatly on the desk in front of him and leaned forward, staring at Al as if he were Moses bringing the Ten Commandments down from the mountain.

Al spoke, and the students listened. They were in the close and holy now, and Al knew somewhere deep in his heart's core that the now was a happy place indeed.

CROP CIRCLES

EVEN HUBERT CRUIKSHANK got caught up in the hullabaloo. He came barreling down the township road in his F150 as though gossip was money, and he just had to spend some. There was a plume of dust rising behind him about a mile long, and the dust trailed him around our clothesline, where my good wife, Mandy, had just hung out the washing. She wasn't too happy to see the dust settling on her damp, white sheets.

The F150 sputtered to a standstill, and Hubert jumped out. He did a hop, skip, and jump across what I call a lawn over to the machine shed, where I was getting the combine ready for her fall duties. I was flat on my back, pushing the nozzle of my grease gun at a pesky nipple, when I saw Hubert's head poking around the big front tire. "Did you hear about Old Man Jorgenson?"

"No, what?" I grunted as green grease squirted sideways out of the gun. "Did he die or something?"

"Better than that," Hubert intoned in a high-pitched hog squeal. "He found a crop circle on his back quarter." Hubert was almost out of breath from his desire to tell the news and his fear that he would be interrupted in the telling.

"Crop circle?" I repeated like I was too stupid to think of any new words on my own.

"Yup." Hubert declared, furiously scratching the whiskers on his recessive chin. "It appears the aliens have invaded."

"Aliens?"

"What else could it be?" Hubert said with a searching look. "The wheat was green, and it was knocked down in a perfect thirty-five-foot circle."

The sun was bright behind Hubert, and I found myself squinting up at him. "Thirty-five feet? Is that the dimension of your average flying saucer?"

"Sounds about right to me," Hubert said. He stared at me hard as though staring gave him more credence. "I'm no expert on these things, but I'd say thirty-five feet is about right for a spaceship."

"In philosophy," I said, "that argument would be called *ignotum per ignotius.*"

Hubert looked at me like I'd just given birth to kittens. "What the heck are you talkin' about?"

If Hubert knew about them crop circles, pretty soon the whole town was going to know about them. He was probably on the phone even before he came to my place, broadcasting the news.

Later that evening I saw a steady stream of headlights coming down the road allowance between Old Man Jorgenson's place and mine. Old Man Jorgenson saw them too, and he crawled into his half-ton and white-knuckled it out to his field at twenty miles per hour. I'm sure the old fart felt like quite the celebrity, giving tours of the site where Martians had landed. I wouldn't put it past him to set up a lemonade stand and start charging admission.

I WAS in the local pool hall two days later because it was raining and I needed a haircut. Glen Stapleton was shooting a game of snooker against Hemi Anderson, and I heard Hemi mumble, "Strange days. Strange days." Conversation puts Glen off his game, so Hemi babbled without surcease. "Martians comin' to Korangar," he blathered. "What'll be next? Newfoundlanders?"

Glen missed an easy bank with the black ball. "Will you please be quiet while I'm shootin'?" he hissed through that metallic sound box they gave him when he had his larynx removed.

"I'm only passing the time," Hemi responded. "God knows you ain't much of a conversationalist." Hemi surveyed the green table for a moment and then pounded a red ball into the corner pocket. "They say Alvin Sparks's wife Sadie was beamed up by them Martians once."

Glen snorted into his artificial voice box; it sounded like a computer passing gas. "They prob'ly beamed her back down when they got a good look at her."

"Not before they done some experiments on her," Hemi said. Then he put the brown ball in the side pocket.

Glen didn't like the way the game was shaping up. "Wish somebody'd beam my wife up," he sputtered metallically, "and keep her fer awhile."

I didn't hear much more of their conversation because my haircut was done, and Jerry, the barber, was just slapping some of that smelly pomade on my head. After that, I went over to the post office and mailed a letter to the government of Saskatchewan. I'd misplaced my driver's licence somewhere—that's what comes of putting your driver's licence in your shirt pocket after the cops have ticketed you for speeding—and I was in the process of applying for a new one.

It wasn't long before a reporter from the Saskatoon *Star-Phoenix* showed up, some young fella with greasy hair and hippie ways. I heard that he made the rounds through the pensioners on coffee row and the ladies down in the church basement. I heard he interviewed Old Man Jorgenson himself and took a picture of the crop circle.

Then he came over to my place. He was kind of full of himself, this young man, climbing out of his Volkswagen Jetta and prancing across the yard like a horse in the Musical Ride. It was early on a Saturday morning, and Mandy was still in bed and I was still in my long johns, sitting at the kitchen table with a cup of black coffee, when I saw him coming to the screen door. His knock sounded like a summons.

I stood in the doorway and scratched my nuts. "You one of them Jehovah's Witnesses?"

"No, sir," he said, and he was about to say more, but I interrupted him.

"You one of them fresh-air inspectors they send out from the university every now and then?"

"I'm from the Saskatoon *StarPhoenix*," he said. He looked like he didn't know whether to smile or frown or steal third base. "Can I come in?"

"Sure," I said. "Long as you're not trying to sell me religion or sprayer parts." I let him inside, sat him down, and poured him a cup of coffee.

"Do you have any milk?" he asked.

"Around here, we drink our coffee black."

He told me that his name was Cameron Something-Or-Other and that he was writing a story about the crop circles on the Jorgenson place. He was interested in anything I had to say about it.

"Don't have much to say," I told him. "Don't know nothing about it."

"Nothing?" he asked, getting kind of fidgety. This kid must have thought he was writing for the *New York Times* or something and that I was a Mafia kingpin, the way he was giving me the third degree. "Didn't you see anything last Sunday evening?"

"Like what?"

"Bright lights in the sky? Anything like that?" He was jotting things down in his little notepad.

Our eyes met for a second, and the air was as thick as the coffee we were drinking. "You don't really believe in that hocus-pocus, do you?" I said.

He smiled like he was the only one who had a secret. "Nah," the kid said. "I think it's bullshit. And I mean to get to the bottom of it." That last bit almost sounded like a threat.

"I'm with you there," I told him. "It's a long stoneboat full of hooey, as far as I'm concerned."

"Well," the kid said, getting up from the table, "it doesn't sound like you have much to say on the subject at the moment. Thanks for the coffee." I don't think he'd had more than a sip.

"Glad to help out any way I can," I said.

He was standing by the screen door, tying the orange laces on his Nike running shoes. He looked up at me kind of slyly. "I'm just curious. Did you never go over there and inspect the damage?"

"Why would I?"

"Oh, I dunno." He opened the door and stood there. "I just thought, since he's your closest neighbour, that you might have gone over to take a look."

"It's a load of pigeon shit," I said, "that Old Man Jorgenson dreamed up to make a name for himself. Why would I want to look at that?" I didn't bother explaining to that smartass kid that Jorgenson and I hadn't been on speaking terms since he shot my dog, Lucky, last spring.

"Dunno," the kid said, a big know-it-all grin on his face. "But my job is to ask."

A LADY from the Crop Circle Society blew into town a few days later. She wore a funny toque that was red, green, blue, and purple. She pasted posters on every wall and power pole, advertising a public lecture on Friday evening in the town hall. The lecture was called "What Do the Martians Really Want?"

I figured I'd better go since I didn't have the slightest idea what Martians want. It had also rained the night before, so my canola was a little tough. Mandy and I sat through the lecture, and we learned a lot. It's amazing the erudition that's out there if you'll only stop and listen to it once in a while.

The crop circle lady never took off her toque. I think she had a satellite transponder in there somewhere so she could track the Martians' every move. She started out by showing us some pictures of creatures from outer space, the way Hollywood imagined them. She said that we too often fall into the habit of imagining Martians as hostile to Earthlings. But what if they were just a bunch of good guys? the lady in the toque asked. What if they just wanted to show us the way to enlightenment and social responsibility?

The government of Canada doesn't want us to accept that there are Martians in the vicinity, she said, because the path to social responsibility takes us down the road to communism. She ended by saying that Martians might well be our best friends. They might be living among us, in plain sight.

The lady in the toque of many colours rented a room above the beer parlour for the next three days. She said something wonderful was going to happen. She meandered around town in broad daylight, holding some experimental device above her head. I think she was measuring our aura.

On the third day, all hell broke loose. A big CBC truck rolled into town. Some slick fella in a shiny suit interviewed just about everybody, from our goofball of a mayor to Old Missus Veterral, who's about as dotty as one of her Dalmatian dogs. I was surprised they didn't let the kids out of school so he could interview them, too.

Right smack in the middle of all that, a busload of weirdos showed up wearing space costumes. They called themselves the Children of Anarchy, and they snaked around town sporting placards that read "CROP CIRCLES: HOAX OR GOVN'T COVER-UP?" and "WHAT THE FEDS DON'T WANT YOU TO KNOW: MARTIANS LIVE AMONG US." In some ways, I thought they were right.

The multicoloured-toque lady set up a music stand in front of the town cenotaph. Cameras rolled as she delivered a speech about what the government doesn't want us to know. Every twenty seconds or so, she paused and pointed an index finger skyward with a reverential look in her eye. "They're coming," she said in a husky voice. "You can't stop them." The Martians were among us indeed.

That night, Mandy and I put our feet up and watched the national news. We were interested to see how our proud little prairie community would be portrayed on the airwaves. "You really should put a stop to this," she warned, as we were hearing the latest about the goings-on in Iraq and waiting for our local bit to come on.

"How am I supposed to do that?" I said. "Them Kurds and Sunnis have been bickering since Jesus was a cowboy."

"You know what I mean," she said, and she gave me a playful little shove.

When the news came on about our quiet little town, I could tell right away it was going to be a letdown. Mister Slick, with his shiny suit, was standing in front of the high school, looking like he had about six feet of blue steel up his ass. He started off with an insult. "Korangar, Saskatchewan," he said. "Home of red-necked farmers outstanding in their fields."

Then Old Man Jorgenson come on the TV set, looking like a fox doctor in amongst the chickens. He wore the brim of his cap at a jaunty angle, the way he does when he thinks he's got the better of you, with an earflap pulled halfway down over his left ear. "At first," he intoned, "I thought it was some kind of late April Fool's joke. But then I saw how perfect that circle was, and I knew it had to be right."

"Do you believe in Martians, Mr. Jorgenson?" asked Mr. Slick. He had a look in his eye that suggested Old Man Jorgenson was three bundles short of a haystack. I almost started to feel sorry for the old man, but then I remembered how he'd shot Lucky and left him on the manure pile to rot.

Mr. Slick also interviewed the woman with the toque of many colours, and then there were some shots of those space do-dos with their placards. Next were some shots of the crop circle from various angles, the wheat flattened in a wide circle, almost as if someone had cut it with a mower. It made the whole town look kind of dumb.

When it was all over, Mandy turned to me and said, "This is getting serious now." She gets this steely-eyed look when she's pissed off, and I knew I wouldn't be getting lucky that night.

A COUPLE OF WEEKS LATER, I was deep into the harvest, so deep that Jorgenson and his crop circles seemed like road signs receding fast in my rear-view mirror. The canola was in the bins, but I still had two hundred acres of wheat in swaths.

It was one of those crisp September mornings when the air is so clear and blue that everything comes into focus. You can actually see better, like all of a sudden you got 20/20 vision. I was out on the combine, plodding through the outside swath on one of them wheat fields. The wheat was tough because the previous night's dew was still on it, so it was slow going.

I saw that Volkswagen cutting across my summer fallow. The car came to a stop at the edge of my wheatfield, and the hippie kid from the *StarKleenex* got out and waved at me. Wheat chaff from the straw chopper caught up to me in the cab as I pulled the big machine to a stop.

The kid climbed up the ladder to the cab and popped open the door. "I think I got it figured out," he hollered over the din of the machine. "I'm going to write another story."

"That's all very good," I yelled back, my noise-reduction headphones around my neck, "but I got work to do." I would have liked to pop the clutch and watch that smartass kid go sailing off the ladder into the stubble. But I didn't. That wouldn't have been nice.

He held the steel cab door open. "I figured you might want to know about it," he shouted. "You're part of the story."

I turned the key on the console, and the combine shuddered and went silent. "I'm part of it?"

"I found this in Mr. Jorgenson's field." The hippie kid reached into the pocket of his coat and produced my old driver's licence. "That's you in the picture, isn't it?"

I tried to pluck the licence out of his hand, but the kid was too fast. "That's mine," I said.

"That's evidence," the kid replied. "You told me you never went over to Mr. Jorgenson's place. You said you'd never inspected the crop circle."

"What's it to you if I did or I didn't?" I asked the kid. I should have just planted my work boot in his belly and sent him sprawling off the ladder.

Mr. *StarPeanuts* grinned at me like he had my testicles in a vice grip. "It'll make a good story," he said. "I just thought I'd come out here one more time and give you a chance to come clean."

"I got nothing to say to you, punk," I told him. "Now get the fuck off my gleaner and get the fuck off my land."

WHEN THE STORY came out a few days later, a perfect storm of soft, fresh road apples scourged Korangar with a vengeance. The headline read "A CIRCLE OF DECEIT." There were some nasty words about me and how I'd likely snuck onto Jorgenson's back sixty in the dead of night with some portable object with which to tamp down Jorgenson's wheat. It appeared, the article said, that I'd tied a rope to a stake in order to create a perfect circle. Honestly, you'd think it was premeditated murder, the way they made it sound. They said I'd refused to comment when I was approached by the newspaper.

At the bottom of the page, there was a photo of Old Man Jorgenson, not so celebratory this time, looking like he'd lost his favourite calf. There was a painting on the wall behind him of an old man with his hands clasped in prayer, and, sure enough, Jorgenson's hands were clasped in front of him on the table, just like the old man in the painting. In the article, Jorgenson said he was heartbroken and "he didn't know why anyone would harbour such a grudge against him." Goodness gracious, you know, it only took a timely photograph of an old man pretending to be pious, and then I was the villain of the piece. Nobody bothered to mention that the old fucker shot my dog!

Young Marlow Yuzdepski of the RCMP showed up at my place that October. The harvest was done, and I was out in the yard draining the radiator on the tractor. Marlow climbed out of his cruiser, adjusted his bullet-proof vest so it wasn't riding up around his neck and choking him, and came sauntering over to the tractor. "It pains me to do this," he said, sounding official and not at all like the guy who plays goal for the Korangar Vikings, "but Old Man Jorgenson won't back down." He put his hand on my tractor tire like he was trying to steady himself.

"Won't back down from what?" I could see my breath, blue in front of me. Winter was on its way.

Marlow looked off into the distance for a minute, like he didn't want to say what he had to say next. "He's pressin' charges for wilful damage to his property."

It was my turn to look off into the distance. "The old bastard shot my collie," I said. "Shot him and left him on the manure pile for the birds to get at him."

The young cop looked like he wanted to sit down on the ground and have a good cry. "There's a law against shootin' dogs out here," he said, "but do you have any proof that Jorgenson is the one that shot him?"

"I didn't see him do it if that's what you mean. Just like he didn't see me makin' that crop circle in his field."

"They found your driver's licence at the scene of the crime," Marlow replied. "And now there's a story in the *StarPhoenix*."

"That don't prove nothin'."

Young Marlow looked as though he'd rather be on the face of the moon than standing in front of me at that moment. "It's my job to inform you that you've been charged under Section 430 of the Criminal Code of Canada," he said, "and that you will be required to appear in court on November twenty-first." He handed me some official-looking papers. "I'm sorry about this," he said. "I don't think any of these charges will stand up in court." And then he walked back to the cruiser.

So now I'm awaiting trial for my gross misdeeds, and I've got all these fresh-air scientists blogging about me on the Internet. One sensitive young lady down in California wrote that I should be shot and pissed upon for what I done. She signed her blog "Moonbeam Captain Crunch."

Shot and pissed upon is one possibility. Mandy's taken to sleeping in the spare bedroom of late, so I feel like I been shot and pissed upon already. I spend my nights reading *The Stranger*, about a guy who goes to the beach and shoots someone. I try to comfort myself by remembering that I haven't done anything that bad. I'm a victim of *ignotum per ignotius*.

I wonder what they'll think when I tell them that in a court of law.

WAR WONTON

ME AND THE boys had heard the stories about old Sam Chin, but we never believed them. How he'd wrestled under the name Genghis the Mongol on the pro circuit. Sure, my old man said, they even broadcast some of his wrestling matches on TV. Sometimes, he fought Archie the Stomper, and those were good fights. He was famous for the sleeper hold and for pretending to shove popsicle sticks into people's eye sockets. The ref would always get on his case for cheating. The ref's name was Al Ermine, that much I remember. The old man said it often enough. When he got caught cheating, Genghis the Mongol would call across the ring, "No cheatee, Mister Ermine!" He sounded like one bad dude.

Personally, I thought the old man was just blowing smoke up my ass. We lived in a tough neighbourhood on the west side of Saskatoon, not tough as in Hell's Angels and guns and knives, but tough the way kids get when there's fistfights on the school grounds every day. Heck, my big sister, Edna, was one of the toughest. I saw her standing toe-to-toe with June Gariepy for the better part of an hour once. She fought her own battles; she didn't wait for somebody to do it for her. If you weren't willing to fight, she told me, the past would come back to haunt you one day.

The minute you walked into Sam's Café on Avenue E, you knew he couldn't have been a professional wrestler. Sam was a chunky guy, okay, but he was only about five-foot-six. He was maybe forty-five years old, but I always thought of him as older. He padded around in these stupid grey slippers he always wore, with an apron tied loose over the grey trousers he probably bought off a sale rack at Steadman's. I never saw him when his shirt wasn't buttoned up at the collar, like a real immigrant. He talked better than an immigrant, though, like he'd learned how to speak English pretty good somewhere along the line. Me and the boys used to hang out at Sam's Café all the time, looking for excitement or girls, and I don't think I ever heard Sam raise his voice while I was in there.

The real legend when I was growing up was a guy named Arthur Grandell. He trained as a boxer five times a week down by the bus yards, and he loved to fight. He'd fought in some amateur matches down at the Arena and won most of them. When he wasn't fighting in the ring, he was fighting everywhere else—in bars, in the street, one time outside a Liquor Board store, where he almost killed a man.

Arthur had grown up on the West Side, just like the rest of us, and just like the rest of us, he had a dad who worked at InterCon, shooting cattle with a bolt gun, coming home angry, and taking it out on the old lady. Following in his old man's footsteps, Arthur took a job down at InterCon, too. He had a mean streak about the length of Twentieth Street. Arthur was ten years older than me, but I don't think he'd ever finished high school. Plenty of guys didn't back then. Just for fun, on Saturday nights, he'd stroll down to Yip's or Jak's and break the nose of some hockey player who looked at him the wrong way. He ran with a bunch of guys from the boxing club, and they were a pretty tough crew.

Arthur Grandell had heard the rumours about Sam Chin, same as the rest of us, and he used to appear at Sam's Café once in a while and poke fun at the old Chinaman. "Hey, Genghis," he'd shout, when us kids were around to hear, "got any popsicle sticks up your sleeve?" Stuff like that. Me and the boys would laugh in that forced way that guys laugh when the thing they're laughing at makes them queasy. Because it was an unspoken rule: you were either on Arthur Grandell's side, or you weren't. And if you weren't, there was no power under the blue sky that was going to save you.

Still, I felt sorry for old Sam. He never picked any fights, and he was always good to my buddies and me. He'd get this puzzled look on his face when Arthur called him Genghis, kind of like he was translating the words in his own mind. Then he'd knuckle under. He'd break into a shit-eating grin and say something dumb. "You tell stories out of school, Mister Arthur," he'd say.

The café was a different place whenever Arthur Grandell wasn't around. It was light and breezy. Sam had those miniature jukeboxes in every booth, and we'd shove in our quarters and listen to the Beatles and the Guess Who. Sometimes, Sam would hire us to do stuff for him, like when he hired me and Willy to paint the false front of his café. Or we would help him unload the McGavin's truck when it came. He'd pay us in Cokes and eggrolls. Nobody ever fought in Sam's Café, not that I can remember. There was something about Sam that made it hard to get mad. He was like a calm lake on a sunny day.

When Arthur came around, though, the air inside the place turned to frost and drizzle, like one wrong word and the wrapper might come off the nut bar. Arthur was like that. You'd just be talking to him, having a normal conversation, and he'd say, "What's your point?" And you just knew that your next sentence was going to be the most important thing you said all day.

I resented how Arthur could say anything he damn well

pleased, and the rest of us had to mind our beeswax. I don't know when it was that I first heard Arthur call Sam a chink to his face, but it became a habit. Even back then, in the '60s, when words like "chink" might still be used in private, most people didn't go out of their way to call a man that to his face. But Arthur Grandell did. "Hey, chink!" he'd shout from his customary booth to the counter, where Sam was dealing with another customer. "Bring me some chicken fried rice!" Sam never answered back, but he got this dark look somewhere behind his eyes.

It all came to a head one night when Arthur Grandell was in a surly mood. I don't know what was eating him. Maybe things didn't go so good down at InterCon that day. He strode into Sam's at about eight o'clock, went to the cooler, and helped himself to a Coke. There was nothing new in that—Arthur was always helping himself at Sam's place—but on that evening, Sam was ringing somebody in at the till, and he called out, like it was a big joke, "You pay for that, Mister Arthur?"

Arthur stopped in his tracks on the way to a booth and stood there with the pop in his clenched fist. He just sort of bristled like a porcupine standing in the wind. "My name is Crime," he said, not smiling and not looking at Sam. "Crime don't pay." Us guys all laughed sort of low, but you could see that something was going on in Sam's head. Arthur went and sat in his booth. "Hey, gook!" he called. "Bring me some war wonton." Sam stood behind the counter, processing this for a minute. "Chop chop, Chinaman!" Arthur shouted. "On the double!"

Sam just turned on his heels and disappeared into the kitchen. I sure didn't relish seeing a man give way to cowardice like that.

A few minutes later, Sam teetered out of the kitchen with a big bowl of hot soup in his hands. He ferried it over to Arthur's booth and set it gently on the table in front of him. Arthur inspected the bowl through piggish eyes. He was looking for something to be wrong. "Where's the shrimp?" he said finally through clenched teeth. "There's supposed to be shrimp in war wonton, Chinaman."

"Shrimp is in the bottom," Sam replied quietly, like he didn't want anybody to hear.

Arthur looked at the soup and then looked at Sam. "I don't see no shrimp."

"In the bottom," Sam repeated. He picked up a glass spoon from the tabletop like he was going to stir up some shrimp with it.

"Get your goddamn hands off my eating utensils, chink." It was one of those moments where the next word was going to be an important one.

"This is war wonton," Sam said, his face blank and uncomprehending.

"No, Chinaman," Arthur hissed, cold as winter. "This is shit." Quicker than my eye could follow, Arthur had the bowl in his hands, and he hurled the soup at Sam. The rest of it I remember almost like it was happening in slow motion, the way regrets come back to you almost like they were a bad movie—the surly look on Arthur's face, the scalding broth in mid-air, Sam raising his arms to protect himself, dumplings and beef everywhere. When the bad movie came to an end, there was broth in Sam's hair and on his white apron. I remember a piece of shrimp bounced across the linoleum and came to rest on the floor underneath my stool. My buddies weren't laughing anymore.

Sam just stood there, broth dripping from his stringy hair, chunks of dumplings and seafood stuck to his apron. I heard him say, "You not welcome here anymore, Mister Arthur."

ARTHUR GRANDELL DIDN'T darken Sam's door for the next couple of weeks. Maybe he was feeling a little sheepish over the way he'd mistreated Sam that night in front of all those people.

I was helping Sam all that summer, doing odd jobs, and one day, after I'd cleaned up the trash in his back alley, I was sitting at his counter gorging on some eggrolls and a Coke. The place was empty. Sam was busy stocking the candy shelves with Cuban Lunches and candy cigarettes. Then I looked up, and I saw that he was just leaning against the counter, peering at me like life was just the way he wanted it to be. "You good kid, Barry," he said in his usual meek way. "You like living here? In this part of town?"

I wasn't sure what he was getting at. "Yeah, sure, I guess."

He smiled gap-toothed at me. "You maybe study hard, Barry? Go to university?"

I shook my head. "Aw, Sam," I said, "I think I've had enough school for one lifetime."

"No," he said. "You smart. You study hard." He went back to stocking the candy counter and me to my eggrolls.

I didn't know how to put my next question into words. I wasn't used to adults taking me seriously, but Sam had opened the door a few inches. He seemed like one of the guys in a way, like he didn't have an answer for every question the way my old man seemed to. "How 'bout you, Sam?" I heard myself say. "Do you like this part of town?"

He peered at me over the counter. "I like it," he said.

"Wouldn't you rather have a café on the other side of the tracks?" I asked him. "Where the rich folks live?"

"No," he said. "I like it here."

This was turning into a real heart-to-heart, and I felt like I should apologize to Sam for the place where I grew up. Me and the boys hadn't always been very respectful. And then there was Arthur Grandell. "I'm sorry about Arthur Grandell," I said in a hushed, almost embarrassed, voice. "He can be a real dork sometimes."

Sam stopped what he was doing and smiled at me in a reassuring way. "Mister Arthur is just unhappy," he said.

I shook my head. "He's been that way since forever."

He got a serious look on his face like he knew what I was thinking. "So I beat up Mister Arthur," he said. "Then what will happen?"

"He wouldn't bother you no more," I said. I wanted to let him know how things worked on this side of town, but I didn't want to make him feel bad.

"Yes," Sam admitted, "but other people would be angry because Sam is a Chinaman." I could see his point. I had no answer for that, only a shrug of the shoulders. "Don't worry about Mister Arthur," Sam said finally, and his voice was like sunshine. "I think he won't come back." He tossed a wet cloth on the countertop and polished it merrily while I cleaned up on the last of my eggrolls.

SAM WAS WRONG, though, about Arthur Grandell never coming back. Seems to me like the past always comes back to haunt you when it's not dealt with the first time.

It was toward the end of the summer holidays, baseball was done with for the year, and a bunch of us guys were spending all our time at Sam's place, trying to forget about the coming horrors of algebra and English lit. It was maybe a slow time down at the boxing club, too, because Arthur Grandell marched into the café one night with three or four of his boxing buddies, each of them looking clean-cut and shiny like they'd just sweated out the last ounce of weakness from their bodies.

"Hey, Genghis!" Arthur shouted as the screen door slammed shut behind him. "Are we cool now?"

The place was pretty full, not just with us kids but also with some older folks having supper. Sam was busy ferrying trays of steaming food from the kitchen to the booths, but he stopped and stared at Arthur. "I told you," Sam said simply, "not to come back here anymore."

Arthur thought he was joking. "Aw, don't be like that," he said more evenly. "Let bygones be bygones." Then he sauntered over to the booth where me and the boys were sitting and shoved a thumb into my neck. It felt like a screwdriver. "What are you doin' sitting here?" he said.

I mumbled something about not thinking that Arthur was ever coming back, and then my buddies and I went and sat on stools at the counter. Sam walked past Arthur back toward the kitchen. "You go now," was all he said.

Arthur's boxing buddies looked at one another like they'd never seen such disrespect for their friend. Arthur just let out one loud German Shepherd bark of a laugh. "Chop suey for me and my buds," he called as Sam exited to the kitchen. "Lickety-split, Chinaman!"

Couple of minutes later, Sam came trundling out of the kitchen with trays in both hands, trays loaded with sweet and sour chicken balls, fried rice and steamed vegetables. I saw Arthur stick his running shoe out to trip Sam up as he made his way around the counter. I remember the running shoe making contact with Sam's grey slipper, Sam stumbling and almost falling but managing to keep his balance—almost as though he'd expected Arthur to be up to his old tricks—gripping the trays deftly in his hands until he got control of himself again.

I'm sure almost everybody in the café had seen Arthur's attempt to trip him up, but Sam went about his business as if nothing happened. He made his way to a table and delivered the food to his waiting customers. Then he came back to the counter by the till, put the trays down, and turned to Arthur. "You leave now."

The place went quiet, and Arthur had that pig-eyed look on

his face. Sam stared hard at him. "What ya gonna do?" Arthur hissed. "Throw a chicken ball at me?"

Sam got this calm look on his face, almost a smile. He reached out for Arthur's hand like he was going to shake it or something. In one motion, he locked Arthur's wrist and raised him up out of his booth to a standing position like he was a dog begging for a piece of meat. Turning his back, Sam leveraged Arthur's right arm over his shoulder, palm toward the ceiling, like Sweet Daddy Siki in the wrestling shows. He tugged downward ever so slightly. I heard a crack like a tree snapping, and Arthur was on his knees, screaming at the sight of his own mangled arm, bent backwards in a way that elbows aren't supposed to bend. "You broke it!" he snarled like a wild cat. "You broke my fuckin' arm!"

Even hurt that bad, Arthur tried to get up, like he was going to fight Sam with one arm and two legs. Sam circled around Arthur calmly, like a wrestler circling his victim before the take-down. It was almost like he was hypnotizing Arthur, the way he never took his eyes off him. There were no popsicle sticks and no turnbuckles to jump off of, no referee to fool with misdirection. It was only Sam and Arthur, who was trying hard to get up off the floor as his buddies looked on. Then Sam had his hands on the collar of Arthur's shirt. Sam tugged the collar gently once, digging his knuckles into the pressure points on Arthur's neck. It didn't look like much more than a gentle reminder that you ought to be polite to people. I saw the colour drain from Arthur's face, the look of disbelief in his eyes before they rolled back in his head, and he crumpled limp to the floor like Archie the Stomper in one of those TV wrestling shows.

One of Arthur's boxing buddies stood up, but he didn't dare come near Sam. "You killed him," the guy said, his face white with horror.

"He's not dead," Sam replied. "Just sleeping."

After Arthur came to again, hissing at his buddies to keep that fucking chink away from him, Sam told them all to leave. They didn't put up any argument. They got Arthur to his feet, supporting him by his good arm like a wounded soldier. They were careful not to slam the screen door when they left.

My buddies and I stayed at the café for an hour or two after that, until we knew our parents would be wondering where we were. We were happier that night than we'd been for a long time, like some huge weight had been lifted from our shoulders, jabbering away about Sam and his exploits and about how maybe he was a pro wrestler after all.

I remember thinking to myself, as I said goodbye to my friends and walked home through the dimly lit backstreets of Saskatoon, that the past comes back to haunt everybody sooner or later. Maybe I would go back to school, I thought; maybe one day I would get out of this town.

BIG OIL

NIGEL KENNEDY WAS LOITERING on the boardwalk, looking at a bulldog decked out in a bikini, when he got the call. He strolled into the white sands of Venice Beach and fished in the front pocket of his Lucky jeans. "Talk to me," he said into his smartphone.

At the other end of the call, Mayne did not bother with pleasantries. "We need you in Libya," he said, his voice remarkably clear (Nigel thought) for having been bounced off numerous satellites all the way from London.

"When?" Nigel's attention drifted to two elderly women in diaphanous gowns who were engaged in an interpretive dance up to their ankles in seawater.

"Yesterday," Mayne said, "if not sooner. McIsaac didn't show."

"I can be there next week," Nigel replied, his rhythms Californian despite his plummy British accent.

"There's nobody cooking out there." Mayne's voice was more urgent now. "I've booked you on British Airways Flight 1239 tomorrow at 8.35 in the a.m.."

"Fuck, Mayne."

"There's an extra thousand in it for you if you can agree with our terms."

When the call was finished, Nigel squinted at the sun breaking through the smoggy California haze in mid-morning. He loved this place.

FIRST CLASS WAS NOT TOO good for Nigel. He'd been flying that way for six years, ever since he'd reached the venerable age of twenty-five. He no longer arrived early so that he could be seated with the other Gold Star passengers, so that he could gaze, with a flute of champagne in his hand, at the plebes as they made their way to the back of the plane. These days, he arrived customarily late, just before the gate closed. He always wore a blazer and a tee shirt when he travelled, as though first class was an everyday occasion for him.

As he was packing his hand luggage in the overhead bin that morning, he noticed a young woman reclining in 3B, perusing some dog-eared pages and sipping an orange juice. She was gorgeous and blonde, almost too skinny. When he had gotten himself seated, and before the canapés arrived, he began to converse. "You a movie star?"

The young woman peered up from the manuscript she was studying. "I'm an actress."

"I'm British," he replied. "We don't make a big deal about actresses where I come from." She smiled vaguely and went back to her reading. "It's a long flight," Nigel added. "I'd appreciate having someone to talk to."

It wasn't until a steward had come through with a breakfast of croissants and orange juice that the two of them spoke again. "I think we've perhaps gotten off on the wrong foot," Nigel said to the actress. "I'm really a nice fellow when you get to know me."

THERE WAS no chance of a layover in London, so Nigel didn't have the opportunity to retrieve his British passport from the flat in Chelsea. He'd been flying on an American passport, made possible for him because his mother was an American citizen. It was less hassle getting into the States with a homeland passport. Although he knew that Tripoli had reason to be suspicious of Americans, Nigel thought that his U.S. passport wouldn't be a problem. He was working, after all, for a British petroleum company. Even the Libyans knew that money made the world go round.

Nigel tried to look confident as he strode into the customs line at Mitiga Airport. The queue was not long. At the customs desk, a grim border officer with a bushy moustache hardly looked at him. The officer perused Nigel's passport. "You are American?"

"Yes."

"You do not sound American."

"I was born in the UK."

"I have to talk to my supervisor," the border officer said. He picked up the telephone and uttered a few words in Arabic.

Moments later, a tall man in a military uniform arrived at the customs desk. "Follow me, please," he said.

Nigel and the tall man proceeded down a grimy corridor to a broom closet of a room with a desk and two chairs crammed into it. The tall man edged around to his side of the desk and asked Nigel to take a seat. "You are here to work on oil rig?" the tall man asked.

"Yes."

The tall man looked at Nigel with eyes that were weary. "There is problem with your passport," he said calmly.

"A problem?" Nigel sputtered. "What problem?"

"Just problem." The tall man waved his hand vaguely. "You cannot enter."

Nigel straightened up in his uncomfortable chair. "Well, that's bloody ridiculous," he said. "I'm here to work for a major oil company."

"Nevertheless," the tall man said with another wave of his hand.

THE FLIGHT back to London that evening was not overcrowded. Nigel spotted three middle-aged men in suits— probably diplomats of some sort—and two close-shaven men he took to be mercenaries or security guards. They were not the most companionable folks with whom he had ever travelled.

He rode the Piccadilly Line from Heathrow to Sloane Square just before midnight and walked through the charmed streets of Chelsea to his flat. It felt good to be back in London, in the heart of England, even in November when the leaves had fallen, and the wind blew briskly off the Thames. It felt good to relax in the soft memory foam of his bed, with thoughts of trendy Sloane Square girls ambling through the backstreets of his mind.

THREE DAYS LATER, Nigel was standing at the customs desk at Mitiga Airport again, this time armed with a British passport. The customs officer, a clean-shaven man in a crisp uniform, consulted the computer screen in front of him. "Wait here," the officer said. He conferred with the man at the next desk for a moment, both of them looking occasionally in Nigel's direction. After the brief conference, the young customs officer returned to Nigel and said, "There is problem."

The words were hardly out of the officer's mouth before Nigel heard the unmistakable thud of military boots running down a corridor. Two swarthy soldiers, their AK47s levelled at Nigel, barked commands in English. "Get down!" they yelled. "Down on the floor!"

Nigel lay on the floor, a soldier's knee in his back, while another soldier twisted his arms and yanked the cable ties tight around his wrists. He knew in his heart that this was just the beginning of a very bad day.

AFTER A BRIEF INTERROGATION in the same small office he'd been in three days earlier, Nigel was hooded and escorted outside to a waiting vehicle. He tried to keep track of the number of times the vehicle turned and of the sounds along the way as the vehicle sped through the streets of Tripoli. The jackhammer clatter of motorcycles and the creaking of auto rickshaws were everywhere. The high, insistent voices of street vendors rose above the tumult, and Nigel surmised that they had passed an outdoor market. After some time, the ruckus outside the vehicle calmed to the whir of tires on asphalt and the low, unintelligible voices of the man beside him and another man in the front seat. The road was rougher now. The vehicle screeched to a stop.

Still hooded, Nigel was led out into what must surely have been the desert. He felt the sweat gather in the armpits of his trendy Camden Market tee, felt the sand crunch beneath his sneakers. He was made to kneel. In his blind terror, almost as in a dream, he heard the mechanized click of a gun being cocked. There was no way to prepare for this, no way of dealing with the harsh truth of it, and Nigel's brain sped into overdrive, a thousand thoughts making it impossible to think one clearly. Venice Beach came back to him, the dog in the bikini, the movie starlet on the plane, his own London flat, the customs officer at the airport.

Loud voices interrupted the cacophony of his thoughts. At least three people were arguing in Arabic, their voices like the voices Nigel had heard on the news almost weekly, celebrating the holy war, promising to fight forever. The argument lasted for some time, voices raised against the desert wind. Nigel waited for the inevitable gunshot.

At last, one of the men grabbed Nigel roughly by the collar of his sport coat and dragged him away while his legs scrambled to keep up. Then there was no earth beneath his feet, and he felt himself falling, falling, with only the hand on his collar to restrain him. With a thwack, his feet felt ground again, and Nigel fell forward onto his knees, his face smashing into warm sand.

WHEN NIGEL CAME TO, an indeterminate amount of time later, he could taste blood. He ran his tongue over lips that felt like sun-cracked leather. The hood still covered his face. He was in a world of darkness. He tried to call out, but all he could produce was a gravelly whisper. "Water," he grated. "Water."

Silence answered him. Nigel felt himself melting into the silence like a cadaver rotting in the earth.

"WAKE UP! WAKE UP!" The voice was strident. A rude hand yanked at his collar. "You wake up!"

Nigel felt somebody pulling at his hood, and, in an instant, it was removed. He wanted to shield his eyes from the light, but the cable ties around his wrists prevented that. "You cannot see me," the voice said, almost jocularly.

Nigel squinted at his new home, a messy six-foot by three-foot hole in the sand. Through swollen eyes, he made out the form of a teenage boy at the edge of the hole. The boy was wearing sunglasses and a baseball cap with a New York Yankees logo on it.

"Water," Nigel murmured.

"Water. Of course." The boy held a canteen to Nigel's swollen lips. "Hey," the boy said, pointing at Nigel's dirty black tee shirt. "You like Mumford. I like Mumford. We trade."

"Trade?"

The boy held his arms out as if to advertise his own Benetton tee. "This good shirt," he said. "Not knock-off. Is good trade." He said it in such a way as to make Nigel aware that the only way forward was to trade.

"When my cable ties come off," Nigel said, "we trade."

"Yes," the boy said. "We trade when the handcuffs are off."

"Where am I?" asked Nigel.

The boy looked around him. "What you think?" he replied. "In a hole. In the ground."

"Why are you keeping me here?"

"You CIA," the boy said.

"No."

"You hungry?"

"Yes."

"I bring food. Later."

NIGHT DESCENDED. Nigel stood up in the corner of his bunker and poked his head out, listening to the papery whir of the locusts. He thought about his apartment in Chelsea, everything in its place, the California King bed, the flat screen TV—all fifty-two inches of it—the kitchen neatly arranged to conserve space. Not far away, sitting in a lawn chair and humming some unknown song, the boy cradled an ancient rifle in his arms. Wagering that an escape attempt would be close to suicide, Nigel sank back down into his grave and drifted off to sleep.

He was still asleep when the boy prodded his shoulder. The boy was wearing a bandolier over his Benetton tee, but the rifle was nowhere in sight. He tossed a cluster of figs into the hole. "For you," he said. The boy climbed down into the crevice and, with a sharp knife, severed the plastic ties around Nigel's wrists. Nigel stretched his arms out to his side. They felt like lead.

It was some time before the feeling returned to his fingers, and when it did, Nigel ate like a man at his last supper. After he had finished, he asked the boy, "What's your name?"

"Mohammed."

"What's going to happen to me?" Nigel asked before shoving another fig into his mouth.

"Why did you come here?"

"To work in the Sirte Basin," Nigel replied. "I'm an oil rig chef."

The boy squinted, looking off in the distance. "What gives you the right?"

"We make money for your country," Nigel said.

"You rape my country," the boy said, looking hard at him. "You confiscate its wealth. What gives you the right?"

A WOMAN APPEARED with two plastic plates piled with rice and goat meat on the evening of the second day. She wore a scarf over her head and a longsuffering look on her face. She handed the plates to the boy, said a few words, glanced briefly at Nigel, and departed.

The boy gave one of the plates to Nigel. "Eat," he said. The plate was still warm.

"Where did this come from?" Nigel asked.

"My mother. She is good cook." The boy sat down at the edge of the hole, placing his rifle on the ground, and ate.

Nigel dipped into the soft, warm rice with his right hand and eyed the rifle. "What do you want to do when you grow up?" If he distracted the boy, Nigel thought, he might have a chance at securing the gun.

The boy looked off at the barren expanse in the distance. "I hope to buy house for my mother one day."

"Doesn't she have a house now?"

"She has house," the boy replied, "but very poor. No running water. Dirt floors. One day, I buy house for my mother with linoleum floors."

Nigel stood up, plate in hand, and edged toward the rifle. "That's all you want?" he asked. "Linoleum floors?"

The boy ate heartily. "My mother wants a floor to wax. She has already bought wax."

"She has?"

"Johnson and Johnson."

"But she has no floor to put it on?" Nigel was three feet away from the rifle now.

"I would not try for gun," the boy said. "I am quick."

Nigel wondered what he had been thinking. What use would the rifle have been to him, out in the middle of God-knows-where?

That night, Nigel did not dream of his flat in Chelsea or of Venice Beach. He dreamed, instead, of a house with no floors, of a woman slaughtering her goats with a machete. When he awoke, he felt that his own aspirations were somehow worthless. He felt cheapened. This teenage boy was prepared to die for what he believed. Nigel wondered what he would be prepared to willingly die for.

ON THE THIRD DAY, Nigel heard two voices arguing. He heard the word "American" repeatedly; the rest was in Arabic. Finally, a soldier stood at the edge of the hole, machine gun in hand. "Come with me," he shouted.

The soldier dragged Nigel out of the hole and escorted him to a waiting van. He pushed Nigel onto a threadbare bench seat and slid the door shut. Nigel could see another soldier in the front passenger's seat, slumbering over an AK47. The first soldier climbed into the driver's seat.

The boy who'd been guarding him came to the window of the van. "Nigel," he said. "We trade shirts now?"

The first soldier barked at the boy in Arabic and sped away.

Churning up dust, the ancient van clattered through miles of red desert. The radio played music that Nigel recognized as Sufi. The soldiers did not speak. Nigel saw the tall towers of Tripoli looming ahead, and then they were passing through squalid suburbs, women and children kneeling expectantly around kerosene fires. Finally, he recognized the international terminal at Mitiga Airport. The van whined to a stop at an entrance with words in Arabic printed on it but also with the English "PROHIBITED."

Nigel was escorted up a set of stairs, and into the customs cubicle he remembered so well. Looking out of place in his crisp Saville Row suit, Andrew Mayne stood beside the desk in the cramped room. "We've had a devil of a time locating you, old flower," Mayne said.

Staring at the man as at an apparition, Nigel said, "You've found me now."

Mayne smiled. "Let's get you washed up and into some clean clothes."

"No need," Nigel said.

"I can't have you walking into the compound," Mayne replied, "looking like you've just spent three days in the chokey."

"I'm not going to the compound," Nigel said plainly. "I'm going home."

IT WAS AN ECONOMY TICKET OUT, but Nigel was thankful for it nevertheless. There were no Hollywood starlets to sit beside, no flutes of champagne to imbibe. A Libyan woman sat in the seat beside him, next to the window. She was holding a baby. Nigel did not engage her in conversation. He was nervous, and he guessed that his nervousness probably showed. The plane had been sitting on the runway for half an hour. Never a religious man, Nigel clenched his eyes and prayed. *Please, God, get me out of here.*

"I'm sorry if the baby cries," the woman next to him said at last.

Nigel pulled himself together. "That's quite all right."

"He needs an operation on his heart," she added. "That is why we are going to London."

"I'm sorry."

The lady covered Nigel's hand with her own. "There is no need to be afraid," she said. "Air travel is quite safe."

"Thank you." Nigel smiled at her.

She gave his hand a polite squeeze as the plane jolted forward. Soon, they were rocketing down the long runway, hoodoos of steam rising off the asphalt. Nigel felt the rush of the plane's engines in the back of his head as if for the first time, as the wheels deserted the runway for the smooth air that awaited. He was still holding the woman's hand as they circled once over Tripoli and glided out over the emerald waters of the Mediterranean.

SIX MONTHS LATER, Nigel had landed a job in a small restaurant in Kensington. It wasn't a particularly well-known establishment, with seating for only fifty patrons, but the menu was excellent, and it gave Nigel the opportunity to experiment with French cuisine. The customers were not movie stars, but they were trendier than Nigel was used to, and he sometimes thought of them as smug and self-absorbed. They were his people, however, and they seemed to appreciate his food.

It was in the middle of a busy evening when the tulips had begun to appear in the parks, when spring had begun to arrive in London in a wet drizzle, that Nigel got the phone call. "Long time no see, mate," the voice said. It was Mayne again. He suddenly sounded far away, although he was likely phoning from his office near King's Cross.

"Mayne," Nigel said. "How can I help you?"

"There's a gig in Venezuela."

"Sorry," Nigel said into his cell, all the while shifting mushrooms and butter in a hot pan.

"I can offer you more money," Mayne said. "Certainly more than you're making in that shitty little restaurant."

"Sorry, mate," Nigel replied. "Money isn't everything." He smiled wanly as he touched the terminate-call button on his phone; smiled as he caught the scent of the rice cooking in the pan.

THE SEWING MACHINE

MAMA SEWED LATE into the night when us kids were in bed. We could hear the clatter of that Singer sewing machine through the hot air grate in the floor. Papa would be asleep by then, deaf to the soft rumble of the machine, to the rhythmic back and forth of her foot upon the treadle. With nimble fingers, Mama threaded the bobbin—I saw her do it many times in daylight—and loaded the spool on the machine. Quietly in the night, she edged calico under the foot press, turned the balance wheel ever so slightly until it matched the motion of the treadle, and she was off in a rapture of creation. She didn't work from a pattern; she couldn't afford it. There was only the cloth and the bold machine and a kernel of imagination. The howling wind that gnawed at the cracked siding on the house, that searched out chinks in the window casings, blew itself out and limped away as Mama sewed.

She sewed any piece of cloth that would hold together. She sewed underwear out of Buckeye flour sacks and dresses out of old shirts. She made blouses out of burlap and trousers out of discarded corduroy. She patched the canvases for Papa's binder with old horse blankets. She sewed my first Sunday School dress out of an ancient bolt of cotton that she'd found in a garbage bin behind the church. Some of her handiwork she sold to the neighbours. Sometimes, she sang a song about a girl named Pearl as she sewed.

Us kids didn't know how bad we had it in 1936. There was always food on the table. We wore hand-me-down clothes, but so did every other kid in the district. I was thirteen and tall for my age—I took after Mama—so I heard more of what my parents said to each other than my little sister, Edna, or my brother, Roy, did.

I remember one night, especially, when Papa and Mama sat at the kitchen table late into the evening. They were mostly in the dark because I had commandeered the coal oil lamp to read by. Papa's voice was pained and thin. "What are we gonna do?" I heard him say.

"Don't worry," Mama said. "Things'll get better next year."

"We got no money," Papa said.

"We still have the home quarter. They can't take that away from us."

"I'm sorry, darlin'," Papa said. "I guess I ain't much of a farmer."

The next day, I watched as Papa took down the barbwire fence on the quarter that he had bought at auction from our neighbour, Mr. McWilliams, ten years earlier. He was prying the fence posts out of the parched ground and loading them on a rack behind old Babe. He carted the posts and wire back to the home quarter and started building a fence there. He told me sometime later that I couldn't go out to the McWilliams place and pick berries anymore. "It doesn't belong to us now," he said.

MAMA DIDN'T HAVE many friends because we lived so far out of town. She especially lacked another woman—someone her own age—in whom she could confide. She sometimes talked to me about her own childhood, how she'd grown up in Colorado and how her own mama died when she was just a little older than me. She told me stories about how brave her mama was when the pain got unbearable, and no surgery would help. "It's surprising what you can put up with," Mama said. "We're all capable of a little heroism. At the right time in the right place."

Annie Hufnagel had been my Mama's one true friend, but she lived two miles away with her own husband and family in a tarpaper shack. When Annie and her family finally pulled up stakes and were going to leave—just walk away from the house and the barn and the land—Mama sensed her world getting that much smaller. She got Papa to hitch Babe to the buggy, and she drove with me to see Annie off. Annie's face was hard as an early frost, like she was refusing to allow the happy memories to creep back in. "We're going to B.C.," she said, her eyes like grey stones. "Maybe we'll see each other again."

"Oh, Annie," Mama said, "I'll miss you so much." They hugged for a long time out there beside the Hufnagel's hayrack, which was piled high with beds and chairs and a table. Words couldn't tell how much Mama would miss Annie.

IT WAS the middle of a summer with no rain when Mama loaded us kids in the buggy and drove into town. Outside Burlington's store, she told us to mind our Ps and Qs. "Mr. Burlington doesn't want children running around his store like a bunch of jackanapeses," she said, "fingering his merchandise."

She knew her little chastisement would be useless, and it was.

Inside the store, Edna fell in love with a doll that stood on a high shelf. Roy had his hand in the apple barrel almost as soon as we were inside. Mama had told me to look after the kids, but I was mooning over a white dress with blue polka dots that was hanging at the far end of the store.

Lucky for us, the store was almost empty because it was so early in the day. Mama gathered up some cornstarch and some coffee, a sack of flour, and a bag of sugar and placed them on the counter. Under the watchful eye of Mr. Burlington, she found a few spools of thread and rummaged around in the bolts of material that were hanging on wooden dowelling in the dry goods section. Greedily, she touched the expensive wool and the gabardines, but she passed them by for the cheaper cottons. She observed the packages of sewing patterns nearby, which displayed the height of fashion in New York and Paris. There would be no market for kitchenette pyjamas or leading-lady gowns or beach-romper bathing suits in Saskatchewan, she knew, but matinee blouses, stardust skirts, capelets, and salon trousers she could sell as soon as she could afford the material. She memorized the drawings on the front of the packages.

I was standing in front of a mirror with the polka-dot dress draped over my slender torso when Mama appeared at my side. "Oh, Mama," I said, "see how pretty it is. Do you think I could have it?"

She smiled at me in the mirror. "One day," she said.

"If we wait till next year," I said, "it won't fit me anymore."

"You really like this dress?" she asked.

"Oh yes, Mama. I love it." The dress had raglan sleeves and a découpe neckline.

She thought for a moment. "Well," she said, at last, "bring it along."

We went back to the fabrics, and Mama picked out a serviceable cotton, the cheapest on the rack, white with blue polka dots. Then we headed to the counter where Mr. Burlington stood, quite dapper and smart. Mama showed the dress to Mr. Burlington. "What's the return policy on this?" she asked.

"Thirty days on all dry goods," said Mr. Burlington. He calculated the prices on a big brass cash register, all the while making small talk with Mama about the farm and the weather. "That'll be seventeen dollars and sixty-five cents," he said at last.

Mama didn't look him in the eyes. "We were hoping," she explained, "that you might extend our line of credit until the harvest is done."

Mr. Burlington looked troubled. "I would like to help," he said, "but I cannot keep carrying everybody's debt. It's been six months, and I haven't seen any payments on the sewing machine or the gramophone or the beds."

"We'll pay you as soon as we can."

Mr. Burlington leaned over the counter and looked Mama in the eyes. "I've heard that before."

"Surely we're not the only family asking you for credit."

I leaned up against the counter beside Mama, and Mr. Burlington looked sheepish when he saw me. "No," he said, "you're not the only ones."

"Just until the harvest is done," Mama pleaded.

There was a long pause. "All right, until the harvest is done," Mr. Burlington said, "but that will have to be the end of it."

MAMA SEWED through the contrary nights, fashioning shirts out of old blankets as the lanterns sputtered around her. The beloved Singer hummed and clattered as the wind blew outside, as a fine layer of dust settled on the windowsills and countertops.

She sewed until she was unable to thread the needle, with dust in her mouth and in her eyes, dust settling on the wooden floorboards like a swarm of termites. She sewed until all thought deserted her.

She wouldn't let me wear my dress, not once, except to try it on for size. She left it on a hanger on a nail on the plastered wall, measuring it with her milliner's tape and then cutting panels from the bolt of cotton she had purchased. She fussed over the raglan sleeves, altered them endlessly.

One bright morning, before breakfast, there were two white cotton dresses with blue polka dots on hangers on the wall. Mama asked me if I could tell the store-bought dress from the homemade one. I couldn't. "Well," she said, "we'll have to figure it out. Because one of these dresses has to go back to Burlington's store."

THE WEATHER TURNED hot a few weeks later. Thunderclouds gathered in the east, dark mansions in the sky, but there was still no rain. The winds raged through the nights, cracked their cheeks against the broken windowpanes, caused the coal oil lamps inside to flicker and wane. By September, the crop of wheat stood burnt in the field, too spindly even to be used as cattle feed. Papa spent hours listening to his records on the gramophone in the living room. I wondered if he was not feeling well. Mama made up for his listlessness, scurrying around the house, making meals, getting us ready for school. I didn't know how poor we were. I went to school in my polka-dot dress, proud as a peacock at what my mama had made for me.

IT WAS a cloudless day in December when the debt collector first appeared. From the kitchen window, I could see him coming a mile away. A plume of dust rose behind his black car. It was the first time in a long while that I'd seen a working automobile.

When the debt collector climbed out of his car, I could see that he was a big man. He was wearing a handsome grey woollen overcoat, and before he donned his fedora, I could see that his hair was clipped and pomaded close to his skull. There was no snow on the ground, but it was cold, and the man's breath seemed to freeze in front of him, like he was breathing more air than he had a right to. Mama told me to go upstairs, but I was too curious. I went and sat quietly in the living room instead.

Mama met him at the door. "Is the man of the house in?" I heard him ask.

"He's tending the cattle," Mama replied.

"May I come in?" His voice was a subdued snarl.

"Yes."

From my perch in the rocking chair, I could see the man looking around, almost as though he expected to see a rifle levelled at him from the living room. He saw me sitting there, but he didn't hold my gaze. When they were settled at the kitchen table, the debt collector produced a piece of paper from his valise. "This is a Notice of Seizure," he said.

"What does that mean?" Mama asked. Her voice was quaking.

The debt collector looked at her hard. "It means that unless you pay your debt within thirty days, I'll be back here to seize your sewing machine, your gramophone, and your beds."

"Did Mr. Burlington send you?"

The debt collector nodded. "And this is a list of items gotten at the general store in town that have not been paid for." He handed the list to Mama.

"We're going to pay the money back."

"You'd better get busy, then," the man said. "Time is running out."

When the debt collector took his leave and was on his way out to the car, I ran to the window to see him go. Papa was coming out of the barn just as the man got in his car, but Papa didn't stop to say hello or anything. He just marched right by the man. He must have known who the man was.

By the time Papa was inside the house and had taken off his coat and dirty boots, Mama was sitting at the kitchen table, looking at the Notice of Seizure. "What do they want?" Papa asked dully.

"The beds and the gramophone," she said.

"The land?"

"They can't take the land," Mama said. "It's our home quarter."

"Anything else?"

"They also want the sewing machine." Mama was as close to crying as I'd ever seen her. "How are we going to make a living if I can't sell my sewing to the neighbours?"

PAPA WAS NOT a man who could easily ask for charity from other people, but he swallowed his pride a few days later and went to the town office to apply for relief. He came back with a tale of woe. "They're out of money," he told Mama. "Everybody wants relief, and now they're out of money."

"That's ridiculous," Mama said. She was standing over the stove, stirring a pot of soup she'd prepared for Papa's return. "The Morleys got relief. So did the Andersons."

"That was some time ago," Papa replied.

"The Morleys and the Andersons are Liberals," Mama said. She was almost ready to throw the soup ladle across the kitchen.

"So they are," said Papa, the way he always said things when he did not want to have an argument.

The next day, Mama bundled us kids up in our shabby winter coats and harnessed Babe to the caboose, and off we went to town, scarves tied over our faces to keep out the cold. She hitched the horse in front of the town office and dragged us inside. Mr. Nordheim, the town administrator, was busy at his desk with paperwork. "My husband came to see you about relief yesterday," Mama said. Her voice was strident.

Mr. Nordheim looked up at her over his spectacles. "The cupboard is bare, Missus Welland."

Mama brought herself up to her full height, which was considerable, and folded her arms. "I've got three kids to feed," she said, pointing at the three of us. "That's Violet. That's Edna. And that's Roy."

"Yes, I know," said Mr. Nordheim.

"I'm not one of those that wears my political stripe on my sleeve," Mama replied, "but I'm not leaving this office without a settlement."

"Now, Missus Welland . . ."

"Either you're going to come through with some money now," Mama went on, "or this town can look after the raising and feeding of my children."

"Missus Welland . . ."

"Don't Missus Welland me," Mama said. "I know this town office is all about greasing the palms of your political friends, and I won't put up with it any longer."

I'd never heard Mama speak to another human being in such a tone before, and it was embarrassing to stand there and listen. A half an hour later, though, we left the town office with a relief cheque of twenty dollars and headed over to Burlington's store.

Mr. Burlington was standing on a stepladder, reaching for a can of strychnine, when the four of us entered the store. "This'll do the trick," I heard him tell another customer. "They carry this back to the nest, and pretty soon, the whole bunch of them are dead." After getting the customer squared away and out the door with his rat poison, Mr. Burlington turned his attention to Mama. "What can I do for you, Missus Welland?"

"I've brought some money," Mama said, "to pay down our bill." She placed the relief cheque on the counter.

"Well, that's wonderful," said Mr. Burlington. He glanced at the cheque, and a troubled look creased his face. "Twenty dollars," he said. "But you owe over a hundred and fifty."

"It's a down payment," Mama said.

"It's not enough."

Mama lowered her voice because there were other customers in the store. "Please don't take our livelihood away from us."

Mr. Burlington looked at her hard. "That's out of my hands now."

IT WAS a bleak Christmas that year, but Mama tried to make the best of it. She found some battered old tinsel in the attic and hung it with finishing nails from each corner of the living room. Papa slaughtered an old hen, and Mama served it with all the trimmings for Christmas dinner. She had a dollar or two salted away in the dresser, and although I heard her arguing about it with Papa, she managed to buy some candles and some raw nuts for our Christmas stockings.

When the holy day had passed and the new year was almost upon us, I heard Papa discussing a move with Mama. It was late in the night, and I could hear them talking downstairs with muffled voices. Likely, they were sitting at the dining room table. "There's no depression up north," Papa said. "As long as there's fish and wood to cut, there's no way to starve us out."

Mama did not like change; experience had made her afraid of it. "Where would we live?" I heard her ask.

"Fred Hogansen tells me there's still homesteads to be had up north of Prince Albert."

"That's a long way away," Mama said.

"We can make it work," Papa replied. "I'm sure we can."

"What will we do with our land down here?" Mama asked. "Just walk away?"

"Yes," Papa said. "We'll just walk away."

ON THE FIRST day of January, the debt collector returned, followed into the yard by a Mountie in his police car and a large truck. They stopped out at the barn to talk to Papa, and then, exasperated and cold in his stylish overcoat and patent leather shoes, the debt collector led the other men into the house. He shoved a piece of paper into Mama's hands. "This is the list of household items we're entitled to," he snarled. The moving men brushed past her and into the living room.

Mama's prized Singer sewing machine had been inverted for storage on its stand. She'd thrown a cloth over it in the hope that it might be forgotten. She leaned on the machine and watched as the moving men took the gramophone and Papa's delight, all of his recordings of New York orchestras playing the latest tunes. Then, the men headed upstairs to retrieve the beds and the bed linens. They hastily dismantled the bed frames, which were too big for the staircase, and brought them down in pieces.

Standing in front of Mama, the gruff debt collector looked over his list. "I think we're all done here," he said as the Mountie looked on from the doorway. "Oh, there's one more thing." He pointed a stubby finger at the sewing machine on which Mama was leaning. "The sewing machine."

Mama did not move. Us kids were huddled around her. It was the right time and the right place.

"I don't believe you heard me," the debt collector said. "We're taking that machine."

"You are not," I heard Mama say in a voice that was not really her own. It was a deep voice, a grave voice.

"It's here on the list," the debt collector said.

"If you're going to take this sewing machine," Mama said, "you'll have to be a better man than me." She rolled up her sleeves.

The debt collector looked at the Mountie and then back at Mama. I could see him sweating, even though the front door was open and the wintry draft was coming in. "Well, if you're gonna be that way about it," he said at last, "I guess we'll just have to leave it here."

WE MANAGED until the spring thaw. I don't remember how except that we ate pigweed and Saskatoon berry preserves. We slept on mattresses fashioned out of old bed sheets sewn together and filled with straw. Papa butchered a chicken each week, and we feasted on that. We still had a stove to cook things on.

In April, we headed north. We loaded up the wagon with the few household belongings we had left, pots and pans, and some of Papa's tools. Papa harnessed the horses to the wagon. Us kids were loaded on the wagon, too, and Papa urged the horses out of the yard. He had a new gleam in his eye, and his posture was more upright than it had been for some time. We were all excited; Mama had been at pains to paint this move as a new adventure. We were going to a land of deep lakes, of stately pines that stretched hundreds of feet into the sky.

Mama allowed herself a smile as she saw the last of her old house, the house that Papa had built for her when they were first married, disappearing behind a stand of stunted poplars. I sat beside her on the back of the wagon, our legs dangling like a couple of schoolgirls. She had her arm draped over the Singer sewing machine to steady it against the jarring of the uneven road as Papa geed and hawed the horses from the driver's seat.

As the last of the farm disappeared, she began to sing a song about a girl named Pearl who was coming around the mountain.

TRAIN RIDE WITH BUSCONI

"THIS IS YOUR ONE CHANCE," Professor Calder told Sally. "He'll be here for that morning to do a Q&A with the students, and then he's taking a train to Edinburgh. You'd better have your ducks in a row."

Her first year as a PhD candidate at the University of London had taught Sally Liscomb, if nothing else, to have her ducks in a row. Hadn't she lined up the funding just to get here, everything from applying for grants from the Rockefeller Foundation to cashing in her RRSPs to hitting her dad up for the shortfall? Hadn't she found a way to pay her tuition, a whopping fifteen thousand American per year, an exorbitant money grab, she thought, but possibly worth the price? Hadn't she booked her own flights and found her own accommodation? Still, she knew that the best-laid plans gang aft a-gley, in the words of the poet, and she'd heard something about Ariel Busconi's unpredictability.

Sally had loved the theatre since she was a child, but her bookish nature and her ungainly body had made her too shy to be an actor. She'd taken an acting course while still an undergraduate back home in the States and had been embarrassed when her instructor imitated her roly-poly walk one day in class. She'd found her niche with the theatre historians instead, studying the structure of ancient Greek theatres and the social mores of nineteenth-century Norway.

When she'd arrived in England for her post-graduate work, Sally was eager to branch out into the relatively new research area of theatre as therapy. She was intrigued by the use of theatre in prisons to help rehabilitate prisoners, but she was also worried about a program of research that would put her in touch with serial killers and rapists. Sensing some reticence, her supervisor, Professor Jonathan Calder, had steered her toward the famous actor/director Ariel Busconi as a valid alternative, in part because Calder himself had some expertise with the Lecoq disciples of Continental Europe and their emphasis on movement theatre and clown techniques.

She got busy, emailing Busconi's agent in Milan about his upcoming sojourn to the British Isles. She started with the usual compliments for Busconi's work, lying about how she'd always been a fan. It would be of immense value to her dissertation, she wrote, if Mr. Busconi could set aside an hour of his busy day so that she could record an interview with him. A few days later, Busconi's agent emailed back: "Dear Liscomb: Busconi in London for one day only. Would be happy for you to join him on train journey to Edinburgh, however, where interview might take place."

Oh, great, Sally thought, *now I'm going to have to add the cost of a railway ticket to Edinburgh and back into my weekly budget.* And what did she know of Busconi anyway? He was in his mid-sixties. In all the photos she'd seen, he was wearing a pair of white tights, leading Italian actors through a series of movement exercises. Perhaps he was a womanizer in the long Italian tradition, preying upon young American women during interminable train rides. She remembered Professor Calder's words, though, about having one chance, and so she signalled her willingness to accede to Busconi's wishes. She would purchase a ticket to Edinburgh for Monday, March 4, she wrote in a return email to the agent, and she would accompany the acclaimed theatre practitioner on his journey north.

In the week before Busconi was set to arrive, Sally purchased her return journey train ticket to Edinburgh, which, to her horror, cost sixty-five pounds. She didn't even want to translate that into American dollars because she knew it would drive her into a blue funk. She recharged her cell phone so that it would be ready when the time came to record the interview. The evening before Busconi arrived, she packed a lunch of cucumber sandwiches—enough for the two of them. Sally went to bed that night in her student lodging, secure in the knowledge that she was as ready as she could possibly be.

ARIEL BUSCONI ARRIVED the next morning with minimal fanfare. Professor Calder met him at Heathrow, treated him to a breakfast in central London, and ferried him across the city to the college. They were just in time for his ten o'clock Q&A with the graduate students.

When Busconi walked into the seminar room, Sally saw a man who, at sixty-five, was vibrant and alive to the roots of his grey ponytail. He moved with the alacrity of a jungle cat, and even when he sat down at the end of the long seminar table, he seemed somehow still in motion, bristling with *joie de vivre*. Sally was instantly as shy as she'd ever been, as shy as she was as a six-year-old on her first day of school. Professor Calder introduced Busconi in a long speech laden with superlatives and noted that it was a mark of the department's reputation that it was able to attract the world-famous actor/director as a guest speaker. He added that he was especially happy to host Busconi since one of his own graduate students, Sally Liscomb, was analyzing the great man's work. Busconi trained his eyes on Sally, who would have melted into her chair if spontaneous melting had been one of her talents.

"It is possible," Busconi said, with a self-deprecating smile, "that Miss Liscomb knows more about me than I know about myself. I think I should leave." He feigned getting out of his chair and leaving, to the merriment of the congregated students. Then he gave a brief introductory statement about his most recent work, not Lecoq-based movement theatre as Sally expected but a newer interest in Sanskrit theatre. He was particularly excited about the Indian concept of the *rasas*. Did the students know that the same word that was used to describe theatrical genres in India was also used to describe the physical sensations of the taste bud —sweet, sour, spicy, and so forth? Busconi argued, in a soft Italian accent, that the equation of physical taste and theatrical genre meant Indian audiences were intended to taste theatre in their mouths. The idea of aesthetic distance would be foreign to a lover of Sanskrit theatre. Busconi was attracted to the idea of that kind of proximity—the in-your-mouth closeness of Indian theatre meant that people could communicate on a more intimate level.

There was a time for questions. Sally's colleagues asked about aspects of Busconi's work, mostly superficial questions that certainly would not be helpful to Sally in her writing. She was heartened by the fact that Busconi answered even the most inane queries with generosity of spirit. Near the end of the session, Sally got up the courage to ask, "What is the difference between being and doing in the mask work of Lecoq?"

"Ah, you see," replied Busconi, "she really does know too much. Being is a state of neutrality, of readiness, of preparing to act. Doing is the action itself. Perhaps we will discuss that further in our interview this afternoon?"

AFTER THE Q&A, Sally rode in the back seat of Professor Calder's Toyota on the way to King's Cross Station. The two men in the front seats spoke to each other in Italian, a language Sally did not understand. When they arrived at the station, Professor Calder said, in English, "I'll leave you in Ms. Liscomb's capable hands, Ariel. Bon voyage!"

Sally's habitual shyness overcame her again as they stood on the platform, waiting for the train. She said little, and when Busconi asked if the arriving train was theirs, she was only able to offer a garbled answer. She was having trouble putting five words together. Her heart was pounding as they boarded the train. None of the compartments in first class were completely empty, so they chose one in which the only other occupant was a young man with a mop of red hair, a ratty coat, and a sullen look on his face.

When they were nicely settled, Sally placed her cell phone on the stationary table in front of her. "I hope you won't mind," she said quietly, "if I record our conversation so that I might quote you accurately in my dissertation."

"Not at all," Busconi said, but his attention was fixed on the red-haired man across from him. Sally looked at the young man. He seemed quite agitated. He was rubbing his forehead with the palm of his hand, vigorously, as though he had some indelible mark there that he wanted to erase. He buried his fingernails in his scalp and scratched with great fervour. When he looked up at Sally and Ariel Busconi, there were tears in his eyes. "Young man," Busconi said at last, "you appear to be unhappy."

The young man stared like a pugilist at Busconi. "I am unhappy," he hissed in an unmistakable East London accent. "I reckon I have a right to be."

"Do you mind me asking what is the problem?" Busconi said.

The young man fidgeted in his seat. "Don't want to talk about it."

Busconi glanced at Sally, then back at the young man. "Sometimes it is best to talk," he whispered.

The young man pointed at the cell phone on the table in front of Sally. "Are you recording this so you can have a sick laugh at my expense later?"

Sally pushed the phone's off button.

"No more cell phones," Busconi said. "Feel free to speak."

"What are you?" the red-haired young man asked. "Some kind of psychologist?"

Busconi leaned forward in his seat. "Just another passenger on Spaceship Earth."

"I hate myself!" the young man blurted.

"But it is silly to hate oneself," Busconi said calmly. "You must love yourself."

"I'm a villain," the young man said. He banged his fist against the metal wall of the compartment. "I'll kill myself when I get up the nerve!" Sally glanced at the young man's knapsack, which was stowed in the open luggage bin above him. Something that looked like the black-gripped handle of a revolver protruded from the open zipper of the knapsack.

Busconi looked at him with a kind, open face. "What is your name?"

"Andy."

"I can already tell, Andy, that you are a sensitive fellow."

Andy was having none of it. He planted his fist into the wall of the compartment again. Sally was startled. "I'm a horrible person," he said, "and I've lost the only woman I ever loved." His articulation sounded like the cry of a wounded animal. Then came the dreadful explanation. "She caught me with her mother!" Andy looked at Busconi as though he expected to see complete censure in the famous man's eyes.

Sally found herself receding into the soft plush of her seat. She suddenly wanted to be anywhere but in this compartment, but some equally strong impulse wanted her to stay.

"Caught you how?" Busconi asked.

"In bed," the young man admitted.

The conversation went on in this vein for a long time. When young Andy showed some signs of calming down, Sally brought a thermos of coffee from her lunch basket and asked the two men if they would like to partake. Both said yes, and both drank Sally's coffee greedily. She had only brought two plastic cups, so she went without while the two men continued their discussion. Outside, the British midlands went rushing by.

Busconi was leaning forward again, earnestly, while Andy was pasted upright against his seat. "Tell me about your father," Busconi said.

"Nowt to tell, really," Andy replied. "He works at the gas plant. Goes to the pub after work every day. Comes home and beats me dear old mum if the lamb is overcooked."

"Do you get along with him?"

"I'd kick the geezer in the Adam's apple if I got the chance," Andy said, and his face got hard again. Sally worried that he would be punching the wall soon. "He last laid hands on me when I was fourteen." Andy's hands were knotted into fists on his lap, but so far, no more wall punching had materialized. "I was holding a saucepan at the time. I informed the geezer that his next blow would be answered with a bang on the head."

More time had passed, and Sally wondered if an interview with Busconi was indeed in the cards. The countryside sped by. Finally, she opened the lunch basket again and pulled out the cucumber sandwiches, neatly wrapped in plastic. Politeness dictated that she would offer the sandwiches to her compartment mates first. They accepted and munched away and talked as the train glided through the hilly farms of Yorkshire. Sally's stomach was growling, but there was no alternative except to go to the concession car, and Sally did not want to miss the chance to begin an interview as soon as the opportunity arose.

Andy was looking much more well-adjusted by the time they were passing through the Lake District. He was making expansive gestures with his hands as he talked. "My first childhood memories are all happy ones," he was saying. Busconi sat beside Sally, exhausted, listening. "I grew up within earshot of the Bow Bells, so how could it be bad? Cockney born and bred. And proud of it."

"Tell me your story," Busconi said, his hands folded in his lap. "The most sane man is the one who knows what his story is."

"You're a kind git," Andy replied. "You are."

"Just a member of the human race."

"I feel better already if you want the truth."

"That's good."

"So, where to begin?" Andy said cheerily. "I nicked me first chocolate confection from a local sweetshop when I was five."

Sally listened as Andy recited the litany of his early criminal activities. There was nothing else to do and little chance that an interview with Busconi would take place. When the train pulled into the station in Edinburgh, Busconi looked drained and unhappy beside her, but Andy was ebullient. The windows of the train car were spattered with rain. The young man sprang from his seat and retrieved his knapsack from the luggage rack above him. He yanked the zipper open, grasped the black-gripped handle, and pulled an umbrella from the knapsack. "It's been a great pleasure," he said to Busconi. "I'm off to the oil rigs. Who needs a girlfriend? I'm me own man now."

As they were alighting from the train together, Busconi turned to Sally and apologized. "I am sorry about the interview," he said. "Perhaps another time?"

"Perhaps." She was almost too tired to care.

"We saved a life today," Busconi said. His eyes were full of sadness and joy.

"Perhaps."

"Well," Busconi said, offering his hand, "I'm off to my next appointment." Just like that, he was gone. Sally watched as he manoeuvred through the crowd and down the platform, watched as his ashen ponytail disappeared among the travellers.

Sally had three hours to kill before her scheduled return trip to London. She walked the Royal Mile in the rain, saw Edinburgh Castle shrouded in fog, toured the building where Robbie Burns wrote "To a Mouse." By the time she got on the train again and had settled in for her long ride home, she had decided that her original dissertation topic wasn't half bad. She would write after all, she told herself, on the therapeutic effects of drama. She had, after all, just seen therapy in action in the hands of a master.

BLOOD-RED POLISH

ON CHRISTMAS DAY, Ester gave the paperboy a lovely box of
sweets. They were maraschino cherries covered in dark chocolate.
She hadn't given me a box of sweets. She'd given me lots of things,
but she hadn't given me that. I imagined the paperboy savouring
those chocolates, the juice of the cherries running down his
pimply chin. I imagined him kissing Ester in the front room, she
leaning into him and cupping his cheeks in her hands.

When the paperboy reappeared at our front door after the
Christmas holidays, I flew at him. I wanted to claw his eyes out.
"You keep away from Ester," I screamed. "You keep away!"

He didn't darken our door for at least three weeks after that,
and only then because Ester called him on the telephone and
asked him why the paper had stopped coming. I was at Ester's
shoulder when she called him, and I heard his every impassioned
word as if he were in the room with us.

"It's Suzie," he said. "She wants to kill me."

"Nonsense," Ester replied. "You're the apple of Suzie's eye."

"She's insane," the boy said.

"Now, Garry," Ester explained, "you know that Suzie is just

high-strung. She's an African Grey. I'll keep her in her cage in the mornings when you come by if it'll make you feel better."

It took a little more convincing, and at last, the paperboy agreed to deliver the *StarPhoenix* the next day.

Hanging up the phone, Ester turned to me. "Now, Suzie," she said, "I know you'd never wish anybody any harm. But you really must refrain from frightening the paperboy."

I cowered a little. "I'll try to do better."

She couldn't help but smile, and when she smiled, my world was full of light. "Who's a pretty girl?" she said.

Ester loved me. I was her only friend, her only confidante through the silent, mothballed days of old age. She could not confide in the paperboy; she could only dress up in her finest woollen dress and her pearls, could only hope that he would notice her miraculous fingernails. He never did.

I used to watch Ester polish her fingernails. She was such a lady. She would assemble the shiny implements of the manicure on the Louis XIV table next to her favourite armchair, the plush velvet one with the doily over the headrest. She would cross her legs in the most seductive fashion. She would pick up the lovely, curved scissors and, with a glance at me, she would clip, clip, clip at the white edges of her fingernails. "When I was a mere sprite of a thing," she would say, "the boys would marvel at the length of my fingernails. I told them that they'd best behave, or I'd use these nails to scratch their eyes out." Then came the file with its incessant *swish swish swish*, almost the sound that a crisp new skirt makes when it is fluttering in the wind. When she screwed the cap off the nail polish remover, I almost swooned. I was intoxicated by the scent. At last, she would apply the blood-red polish in slow, long, ecstatic strokes.

LATER ON, in the cold, wet days of March, Ester was looking at the obituaries. Her face went grey. Ester was in the habit of reading the obituaries to me. "Poor Sadie," she said on that crisp morning. "She was the richest child at my school when we were girls. If you knew Sadie then, when she was a girl, you would never have thought about death and dying." Ester read me the bit about Sadie being mourned by her loving husband of sixty-two years, Dr. Henry Morrison. Then she put the paper down on the Arborite countertop and stared at the bleak day outside her window.

Ester was a changed person after that. She kept the curtains closed in our little house, almost as if she wanted to keep an unwanted visitor from peering in. She sometimes wore two sweaters for fear of catching her death from pneumonia. She was preoccupied by her own mortality, convinced (and perhaps rightly so) that she did not have long to live.

About a week later, we were watching *The Planet of the Apes* on her old Electrolux television—the original version of the movie, with Charlton Heston as the last man on earth. Ester almost swooned. "They don't make them like him anymore," she said. "Now, there was a man who stood by his principles." At the end of the movie, Charlton discovers the hand of the Statue of Liberty protruding out of the sand, and he cries out in fury to the many generations of lost humanity. "You fools!" he cries. "You threw it all away!"

Ester was shaken. She turned to me, her eyes reddened. "No one wants to be left behind," she sobbed, her voice hoarse with emotion. "No sensate human being, at any rate."

She put her life in order the next day. Ester was too frugal to waste money on lawyers, so she set about preparing her own Last Will and Testament at the kitchen counter. She recited the articles of her bequests aloud as she composed. I was heartened to hear that the lion's share of Ester's fortune would go to me, to my care and maintenance, with only a small pittance of five dollars per week going to Garry the paper boy until he reached the age of majority or married, whichever came first. Ester got perceptibly cheerier as she wrote as if she was enjoying planning her own funeral.

I found it curiously unsettling. She was happily divesting herself of all earthly accoutrements and closing the account on the few relationships she had left. I couldn't help but feel that, once again, I was going to be the one left behind, just as I had been by my patron Gertie in another lifetime. Gertie came to a sad end, but I digress.

That afternoon, Ester plastered on her makeup, donned her woollen dress and pearls, and went downtown.

I didn't see her again until after supper. When she got in the door, she announced that she'd had a wonderful meal at the Chinese café down by the bank. "I've brought you some Chinese food, Suzie," she said. "Come have a bite to eat." She spooned some food into a Styrofoam bowl on the kitchen counter, and I enjoyed the repast almost as much as she had done.

She chattered on happily as I ate. "I've just spent the most charming afternoon at the Golden Meadows Sunset Home," she said. "Oh, Suzie, you should see it! Wall-to-wall carpet, walk-in bathtub, everything a woman could want. There's a grand dining room with hardwood on the floor. Big enough for my entire dining set, sideboard and all. And the best part is, it's all covered by the old age pension."

I voiced my immediate disapproval. "But you don't need an old folk's home. You're doing very well here with me."

Ester was adamant. "I'm not much of a cook anymore, Suzie. I really can't fend for myself."

"I'll do the cooking."

"Now, Susannah, you know you can't cook."

"I'll learn!" My voice was suddenly strident. It surprised me, but it shouldn't have done. It was the tone I took toward my last mistress in her final days.

Ester laughed softly, like Lana Turner in *The Postman Always Rings Twice*. "Calm down, Susannah. Everything will be all right." And then she added, a little wistfully, "My only sadness is that they do not allow pets in the building."

ESTER WAS a regular gadfly after that, cavorting about town like a randy widow. She was making a spectacle of herself. Something had to be done.

I was desperately bored while she was away. Something happens to me when I'm left alone for days on end. I get stir-crazy. I start to think strange thoughts. I start to think about mayhem. My mind kept wandering to thoughts about Gertie, my first mistress, and how she finally succumbed. Dead in her own bed, with her heart torn out of her body.

All I could do was watch movies through the endless days. The movie channel was playing old horror films that spring. I saw Alfred Hitchcock's *The Birds* one afternoon and learned that even sparrows have feelings. The next day, *Strait-Jacket* was playing. I gloried in Joan Crawford's frenzied portrayal of a jilted wife. We sometimes kill the things we love. That's what the movie said.

When Ester got home that night, my head was full of Joan Crawford. I could do nothing but repeat the skipping rope rhyme that was immortalized in the motion picture. "Lucy Harbin took an axe and gave her husband forty whacks," I sang. "When she saw what she had done, she gave his girlfriend forty-one."

"That's a terrible song, Suzie," Ester scolded while divesting herself of her coat. "Why don't you sing the theme from *Gilligan's Island*?"

"Lucy Harbin took an axe and gave her husband forty whacks!"

"You're angry because you haven't been fed." She opened the thin wire door of my cage and sprinkled some birdseed into my dish. In her haste, she forgot to shut the door again.

I refused to eat. "Lucy Harbin took an axe and gave her husband forty whacks!"

"Well, if that's the way you're going to be, I'll just have to ignore you." Ester walked right by me and went into the bathroom.

"When she saw what she had done, she gave his girlfriend forty-one!"

"Really, Susannah," Ester shouted over top of my tuneless singing, "you have become quite intolerable these last few days."

"Lucy Harbin took an axe and gave her husband forty whacks!"

"If you'll calm down, I'll tell you some happy news."

My song ended; I needed some happy news.

"I've taken care of every detail," she shouted cheerily from the bathroom. "You will not have a worry in the world when I'm gone."

Ester came back into the living room and laid out her scissors, file, and nail polish on the side table by the plush velvet chair. She sat down and began clipping her fingernails. Clip, clip, clippity, clip, now she's got you on her hip. "Have you ever heard of a place called Parrot Island?" she asked idly. "It's a place where parrots go when their mistresses are no longer capable of caring for them."

She began filing her nails. It sounded to me like chalk screeching across a blackboard. "It's such a lovely place," she continued. "On ten acres of land outside the city. A heated barn where all the birds are kept." She blew the fingernail dust across the room at me. How unsanitary! "There are parrots, budgies, lovebirds, you name it. An old farmer with an eye patch comes out and feeds you twice a day. And at night, he brings along his ukelele for a sing-song."

I was already light-headed when she opened the bottle of nail polish remover. The room began to reel; it was like a flashback episode in *I Dream of Genie*. I thought I was going to be sick. I knew I was going to be angry at Ester's matter-of-fact tone as she outlined my future in glowing detail. *Why not just leave me on a shard of ice in the Saskatchewan River? I thought. That's the kind of respect we have to look forward to when we get old.*

"Parrots almost always outlive their mistresses," Ester said. "Did you know that Sir Winston Churchill's parrot is still alive?" She chuckled to herself. "And such a foul mouth he has on him!"

I'll show you a foul mouth, I thought. I've seen Sam Peckinpah movies too.

Then the bloody nail polish came out. Ester stared right through me for a moment, almost daring me to commit an extreme act, and then she brushed the polish on as thick as scabs on self-inflicted wounds. "You will be looked after," she said. "I've signed the contract this very day." She blew on her nails as if she no longer had a care in the world. "They'll drop by and pick you up next week."

She gave me another piercing look, chuckled her self-satisfied chuckle, and said, "There. Lovely. Haven't I got the loveliest fingernails in the world?" She clicked her thumbnail against the fingernails on her left hand, a systematic display of dominance.

The room stopped whirling at that moment, and I saw every-thing—my life and hers—with extreme clarity. This was no happy-ever-after *Brady Bunch* episode. This was *Strait-Jacket*.

"Kill," I screeched, shrill even to my own ears.

Ester looked up at me. "Susannah? What on earth did you say?" Her eyes were not her eyes. They were the terrified eyes of Joan Crawford, wide and full of death.

She did not have time to chastise me further. I knocked open the flimsy door to my cage. "Who's a pretty girl?" I screamed. "Who's a pretty girl?"

I flew at her, flew at her eyes, pierced them as they had pierced me. I plunged my sharp talons into the soft irises. Vitriol fluid spurted from her eyes like oil from a drum. I plucked out her eyes and ripped open her woollen dress.

PARROT ISLAND IS A LOVELY PLACE. I have a hundred and fifty new friends, all numb to their fate. They wait and they wait for their pathetic lives to end. For the time being, they are content to sit beautifully in their cages. Gawking schoolboys point at them and shout, "Polly wanna cracker?" at the top of their lungs. When they appear before my cage, I click my blood-red talons against my foreclaw, like Ester used to do after she'd polished her nails. The children don't stay long to gawk at me.

We sing the theme from *Gilligan's Island* in unison every night while the one-eyed farmer strums his ukelele. We also sing the greatest hits of the Muppets. I'm heartily sick of "The Rainbow Connection."

I don't like the one-eyed farmer. He has alcohol on his breath, even in the early hours of the morning. Sometimes, he dons an eye patch and dresses up like Long John Silver. Then he parades around the Quonset with one of us on his shoulder, mumbling "Pieces of eight! Pieces of eight!" to the delight of the misbehaving school children.

Someday, the one-eyed farmer will have to die. Someday. None of the parrots like him. We are every one of us alone, every one of us searching for the hand of the Statue of Liberty in the sand.

THEORY OF EVERYTHING

RAY SAT IN THE NISSAN, staring down at the steering wheel as the woman railed at him. "I'm going to report you to the police," she yelled. Part of him wanted to protest, to yell right back at her. He was parked in a public lot. He had just as much right as the woman and her young son to be there.

Still, he sat, looking down at the Nissan symbol on his steering column. "I was—I was trying to be nice," he murmured through the open driver's-side window.

The woman was making a spectacle of herself, standing there in her pink bathing suit and her broad beach hat, waving the red wrapper of a KitKat bar above her head. "You don't just offer chocolate bars to five-year-old boys," she hissed. A crowd was beginning to gather at the far end of the lot, adults and children alike, boogie boards under their arms, gawking at Ray and the woman. Her mouth was a Charlie Brown dash across her face. "I'll let it go this time," she said at last, "but if I see you in this park luring kids again, I'll see your butt in court." She hurled the chocolate bar wrapper at Ray's face, grabbed her stunned little boy by the arm, and stalked off across the parking lot in an explosion of pinkness. The crowd began to disperse, but not before giving Ray and his car the once-over.

Ray rolled up his window and locked the doors. He hadn't been luring anybody for crying out loud. What kind of a place was the world becoming when you couldn't give a kid a chocolate bar? He gazed out the windshield at the sea and at the hordes of people who frolicked on the white sand in front of it. Some people are waiting for the sun to shine, he thought, and some are waiting for that big ball of flame to go out.

THE NEXT MORNING, Ray awoke with a crick in his neck. He'd forgotten to recline his seat as he was falling asleep the night before and had rested his head on the steering wheel, thinking he was only going to nap for twenty minutes. Now, he was paying the price, doing some driver's-seat calisthenics to keep his neck from seizing up.

When he was properly limbered, Ray popped open the door of the Nissan like he was prying open a casket. He needed some air. He got out and steadied himself against the car until his light-headedness faded. Throwing open the hatchback lid, he rummaged through the mess of clothing, utensils, barbecuing equipment, and fishing gear for his coffee maker. He stumbled toward the public washrooms, filled the carafe with tap water, and headed back to the car. He worked up a sweat, getting his little orange generator to start.

After the coffee was made, he stowed his belongings inside the hatchback and strolled down to the beach, travel mug in hand, to watch the ocean. He felt out of place in his khaki trousers and his Mariners baseball cap, the last vestiges of a former life in another city. The sand was sticking to the tube socks in his open-toed sandals, and the socks were bunching up. The locals, tanned and barefooted and out for their morning sun salutations, seemed infinitely more comfortable.

Ray found a piece of driftwood to sit on. The coffee didn't taste half bad, and he was enjoying the clear sky and the rolling waters of Kailua Beach when he caught sight of the crazy kid on a height of land. The kid was sitting cross-legged under a koa tree, his hair straggly and matted, his feet bare. Ray had seen the kid under that same tree every morning for the past three weeks. He was wearing tattered blue jeans and a ratty brown tee shirt. His face was weathered and blotchy. Although the ravages of a life lived in the out-of-doors made the kid look older, he was probably only twenty-one or twenty-two.

With the forefinger of his right hand, the kid was scrawling something in the air in front of him. Was he conducting a symphony of sand, wind, and sea? Or was he working out some intricate mathematical equation? Now and then, the kid would draw an imaginary circle around his imaginary work and slash through it with one brisk, unhappy karate chop. Then, disgruntled but determined, he would start again.

It was one of those things that Ray wanted to look at and that he didn't want to look at. The kid was in a state of turmoil. How was he able to live out here in the elements? Ray could manage because he was a man of means. He had a bank account. Living out of his car was a choice for as long as the money lasted. This kid didn't look like he could negotiate his way into a bank.

Ray didn't have any children—heaven hadn't blessed him that way—but he thought of the crazy kid's parents. Where were they? Why hadn't they intervened in the kid's life? Part of Ray wanted to take the kid under his wing. Another part was screaming no. "Don't get involved," it said. "These things always come back to bite you in the ass."

Downing the last of his coffee, Ray hastened toward the public washrooms for his morning dump.

THE GOATFISH AND the awa weren't biting that evening, but Ray persisted. He enjoyed basking in the warm February moonlight and listening to the shushing of the waves. He was never entirely happy these days, but what more could he want? He was sitting in his folding canvas chair with a cup of homemade hot chocolate in his hand. His fishing rod, anchored into the warm sand, was bending to the tension of the line. Up in one of the pavilions above the beach, some high school kids were passing a joint among them and speaking in the long vowels of surferdom. Everything was stoked and righteous as far as those kids were concerned.

"Fishing," a voice said, guttural, like a voice that hadn't been used in a long time.

Ray almost spilled his hot chocolate, jerking his head around to see who was standing behind him in the dark. It was the crazy kid. He peered at Ray as though he were looking out of a cave. The kid's skinny body had the shape of a bow. His head and his feet were curious, but his torso was afraid. Ray collected himself and said, "Yes. I'm fishing."

The kid didn't move an inch. "Fishers of men, fishers of men," he chanted. "There is no beginning, and there is no end."

Getting up from his canvas chair, Ray stood as tall as a man who was five foot seven could stand. He thought the kid might have a weapon, and he wanted to make himself as big as possible. "Are you okay?"

An angry finger pointed at him. "How many fish are in the sea?" the kid asked. Then he backed away into the darkness.

Ray watched as the crazy kid threaded his way up toward the public washrooms and stopped to drink from the nozzle of the outdoor shower. The kid was talking to himself as he continued through the park, gesticulating wildly. When he passed the pavilion where the high school kids were hanging out, the potheads taunted him. "Hey, hobo clown!" they shouted. "Stay the fuck out of our park!" The crazy kid shouted something indecipherable back at them and made his way to a park bench down the beach.

THE KONA WINDS arrived the next day, bringing with them grey fog and torrential rain. Ray had no choice but to stay in the Nissan most of the day, listening to golden oldies on the radio. Eventually, he summoned up the energy to start the generator and boil some Kraft Dinner on the hotplate. By nightfall, the winds were howling across the beach from the west. The car rocked, there in the parking lot, with each gust.

Through his rain-soaked windshield, Ray could see the outline of the crazy kid. He was lying on the bare cement in the pavilion where the pot smokers had taunted him the night before. His knapsack was under his head, like a pillow, but the kid's feet were bare, and his tee shirt was too thin to keep out the cold. He lay there for an hour, huddled, the wind buffeting him, the rainwater creeping across the cement toward him.

Finally, Ray could no longer justify his own comfort against the crazy kid's lack of repose. He crawled out of the Nissan and fought his way across the lawn, leaning into the barrage of rain. When he was under the roof of the pavilion, Ray bent down to get a better look at the kid. He was shivering, his eyes closed tight against the cold. "You better come with me," Ray said.

The kid looked up, startled. His teeth were chattering.

"You better come inside." Ray helped the kid stand up. He took the knapsack in one hand and supported the kid with the other all the way back to the car. The kid's gait was as halting as an eighty-year-old man's.

When they were finally inside the car—Ray in the driver's seat and the kid in the passenger's seat beside him—the kid sat motionless for some time. He was breathing laboriously. Ray surmised that the kid had a lung problem. He started the engine and turned on the heater. Then, it became apparent that the kid was staring at the photograph on Ray's dashboard. "Who's that?" the kid asked, pointing a trembling finger at the photograph.

"My wife," Ray said.

"Where is she?"

Ray peered at the kid's sunburnt and scabby face. "She's dead."

"Is it God, or is it randomness?" the kid asked. "What do you do for a living?"

"I used to be an undertaker."

"In love with Death," the kid said.

Ray looked at the rain, wondering how to keep the kid from riding off in all directions to Crazytown. "My name is Ray," he said.

Then the kid was writing random numbers in the air in front of him and saying them at the same time. The purposefulness with which he went about this process made Ray believe that there was some method in it. "Three point one six two . . . three point three one seven . . . three point four six four . . . three point six zero six . . ." Ray could see that the kid was getting sleepier as he tried to remember the numbers. In the fours, the kid began to hesitate and falter. Maybe this was his way of putting himself to sleep. "Four point two four three . . . four point three five nine . . . four point four seven . . ." The kid's shaggy head fell forward against his chest. His parched lips continued to move for a while. Now and then, Ray could hear a whispered number, but soon, the whispering was replaced by a soft snoring.

Ray sat looking at the kid as the rain machine-gunned on the roof of the car. The kid had his arm draped possessively over his wet knapsack. As he slept, the kid slouched against the passenger's side window, and his arm fell away from the knapsack. Ray didn't like snooping through other people's belongings, but he also thought that some good might come of knowing the kid's personal circumstances. Maybe there was a phone number for the kid's parents inside the knapsack.

The crazy kid was snoring loudly now, pausing only to cough occasionally in his sleep. When it seemed that the kid was sleeping as deeply as he was going to, Ray wrested the knapsack from his side. He unzipped it slowly and began to look through it. He found a ripped flannel shirt, some chewing gum, a jackknife, and an empty pill bottle with a prescription for methadone on the outside of it. The name on the prescription was Keali'i Williamson. There was also a book at the bottom of the knapsack, a dog-eared copy of something called *The Theory of Everything*.

The kid stirred in his seat, and Ray quickly zipped up the knapsack and rested it on the console between them. He wondered about the methadone and the significance of the book. He didn't think it would be possible to sleep with a methadone user in the car beside him. As the car began to heat up, the kid began to smell like he was moulting. It was the smell of salt and feces and body odour, all wrapped up in mildewed denim.

"YOU STOLE MY UKULELE!" The kid was gesticulating wildly when Ray awoke with a start. The first low sun of morning assaulted Ray's eyes as he tried to focus. The kid's arms were flailing like the arms of those wind turbines Ray had seen at the Dole Plantation.

"You didn't . . . you didn't have a ukulele," Ray blurted.

The kid was clawing at the air between them as though he wanted to hurt Ray but couldn't get near him. "You stole it!"

Ray popped the lock on his door and sprang out of the car. The kid was banging on the dash, causing the photograph of Ray's wife to fall on the muddy carpet of the car's floorboards. Ray scurried around to the passenger's side and threw open the door. "You have to go!" he shouted. The rain had stopped. Ray was glad that it was still early and that no one was around. "You have to go now!" The kid clawed at Ray's wrist as Ray grabbed him by the hair and yanked him out of the car.

The kid was on the ground, clutching his knapsack to his chest. "I want my ukulele back!" He sounded like a wild boar being killed up in the mountains.

Ray was already back in the driver's seat when the crazy kid got up and started banging his fist against the windshield. "You stole my ukulele!" he shouted. The kid tried the door handles, but Ray had locked them. Ray twisted the key in the ignition and lurched out of the stall with the kid coming after him. Shoving the gear shift into drive, Ray narrowly missed running over the kid on the way out of the parking lot.

Ray was still talking to himself when he pulled out on the Kamehameha Highway. He was going seventy-five in a sixty-mile-per-hour zone. He took the North Shore turn-off. He knew that he would be in Haleiwa before noon.

RAY HAD OCCUPIED a parking spot just off the highway along the North Shore for at least a month when a cop stopped to talk to him. It was dusk. Ray was sitting in his canvas chair beside the Nissan, enjoying the crashing waves. The policeman pulled up in an unmarked SUV and asked to see Ray's driver's licence. He walked around the car, shining his flashlight in the windows at Ray's belongings. "This is not a campsite," he said finally. "It's for day parking only."

Ray stood there, watching. "There are no signs about parking here at night."

The cop shone his flashlight in Ray's face. "No sign is necessary," he said in a crisp voice. "It's just common sense."

"I'll pack up and be gone tomorrow," Ray offered.

"You'll pack up and be gone tonight," the cop said. "Vagrants aren't welcome here."

"I'm not a vagrant," Ray argued. "I've got a bank account."

"You've got a bank account?" The cop's smile was wry, cynical.

"Yeah."

"Then why don't you use it to rent an apartment in Honolulu?" The cop gave Ray a steely look. "I'll be by here again in a couple of hours. You'd better be gone by then."

RAY STEERED the Nissan into the Kailua Beach parking lot just before dawn the next morning. He could see the crazy kid perched on his height of land, overlooking the Kaneohe Hills and the ocean, when the sun began to rise. The kid was up to his usual antics, drawing numbers in the air as though he were trying to work out a theory of everything. Ray imagined that the kid, burned out on drugs as he likely was, could remember nothing but his precious numbers. He would probably have forgotten that Ray had tossed him out of the car a month earlier.

Strolling down the beach with his coffee in hand, Ray nodded at the crazy kid, who peered back at him as one might look at a stray dog. Then the kid went back to his mathematical equations. The kid's appearance was even scruffier than usual, and Ray surmised that the intervening month had not been good to him.

Ray found a desiccated tree stump to sit on. He watched the

sea and thought about the stock market crash of 2008. *Yup*, he said to himself, *I'm just here waiting for rigor mortis to set in.*

THAT NIGHT, Ray was awakened by a ruckus down in the pavilions. The voices were young and high-pitched, almost jubilant. At first, Ray thought that it was just high school potheads partying, but he could see from his stall in the parking lot, by the fingernail of a moon that was in the sky, that something else was going on. There was a gaggle of teenagers, maybe six or seven of them, in a rough circle inside the pavilion. In the middle of the circle was the crazy kid, lurching about like a blinded hawk. When he neared the periphery of the circle, a pothead would shove him back in. Ray resisted the urge to get involved. He watched as the violence escalated, listening to the guttural exhalations of the crazy kid as he was pushed about. When he saw the tallest pothead level a punch at the crazy kid, knocking him to the cement floor of the pavilion, Ray lowered his window slightly. Ray had never been in a riot before and had never had occasion to be pepper sprayed, but he could feel something stinging in the air that he presumed was pepper spray. He could hear the taunts of the potheads more clearly now. "Disappear, Hobo Clown!" they were yelling. "Don't come back!"

It wasn't like Ray to get involved, but he couldn't sit and watch as a helpless kid was beaten. Ray opened the door and got out of his car, fifty feet away from the pavilion. "Leave him alone," he growled in a voice that he hardly recognized.

The potheads turned and stared Ray down. "Stay out of it, old man," the tallest one said. "This ain't your business." He kicked the crazy kid in the belly to punctuate his statement.

For a moment, Ray's knees weakened, and he leaned against the roof of the car. He took a breath and thought about the crazy kid's parents, who didn't know where he was. Fumbling to open the hatchback of the Nissan, Ray found a tire iron, smooth and cold to the touch. He squeezed it in his right hand like a tube of toothpaste as he walked hesitantly toward the pavilion.

The potheads left the crazy kid on the cement and moved like a silent army of zombies toward Ray. They met him out on the grass. "What do you want, old man?" the tallest one brayed. Ray could see him better now, a good-looking kid in board shorts and a hoodie, the kind of kid who probably played football on the high school team. How could such a kid be so cruel?

"Who do you think you are?" Ray hissed.

The tall one turned to his buddies and offered up a humourless laugh. The others followed suit, guffawing but not smiling. "We're the Sanitation Department," the tall one said. "We're here to clean up garbage."

Ray pointed his tire iron at the tall kid. His back was against the proverbial wall. "You can start by getting out of here now."

"And you can kiss my ass." The tall one, out of arm's reach, raised an aerosol can. Ray stepped forward, dodging the spray, and lashed out with the tire iron. He managed to connect with the tall kid's extended arm. He could hear a crack that sounded like wood being chopped. The kid dropped his canister in the grass and fell to his knees. He was looking at his forearm in disbelief. Ray could see that the forearm was bent at an odd angle.

Then the tall kid was sobbing. "You broke it!" he whined. "You broke my arm!"

Ray pointed the tire iron at the tall kid's buddies. "You're next," he growled, "if you're not gone from here now." The potheads stood their ground for a moment, staring down at their whimpering leader. "Anybody else want this?" Ray yelled, lifting the tire iron over his head.

Almost as though they'd all come to the same conclusion at the same time, the potheads moved to help their buddy up off the grass. With a host of withering glances toward Ray, they headed off toward Kanailoa Road. When they were on the bridge, past Buzz's, one of them turned and shouted at Ray. "We'll be back, asshole!"

Ray watched them evaporate into the dark. Then he took a breath and walked over to the pavilion. The crazy kid was sitting up now, but he looked dazed. His tee shirt was ripped. Snot and blood glazed his face. He was rubbing his eyes like he was scouring a cast iron pan after a fish fry. There was a gash running down the kid's forehead from his scalp that needed medical attention. Ray knelt beside him.

"Leave me alone," the crazy kid moaned. It was the pathetic, submissive moan of somebody who had lost everything.

There was a jackknife on the cement floor beside the kid. Ray shoved it into the kid's backpack and slung the backpack over his shoulder. "I'm here to help," Ray said.

"I can't see."

"I know," Ray replied. "Let me help you up." The kid let out a pained groan when Ray pulled him up by one arm to a standing position. He threw the kid's arm over his free shoulder and walked him to the car.

A HALF-HOUR LATER, they were standing at the emergency registration desk of Castle Medical. Ray half-expected to see the tall pothead there with his broken arm, but he'd chosen the hospital because he knew there was a likelihood that the kid had gone to a twenty-four-hour medi-clinic nearer the beach.

A nurse was asking the crazy kid for his health insurance card. The kid just stood there, looking like he didn't know whom to trust. "His name's Keali'i Williamson," Ray offered. "That's as much as I know about him. Some kids were beating on him in the park."

The nurse looked at Ray sternly. "We'll need his insurance card."

"I'll pay," Ray said.

"Fair enough," the nurse replied. "We'll need you to sign some forms. And we'll require payment in advance."

IT WAS three in the morning by the time the kid was sewn up. He was looking a little better when he came out of the doctors' area, although his left eye had begun to swell and blacken. Ray loaded him in the Nissan and drove back toward the city's business district. "Where would you like me to drop you?" he asked the crazy kid.

The kid's response was almost automatic. "Kailua Beach Park," he said, almost as though Ray wouldn't know where the beach was located. He was rummaging through his backpack as he said it. The kid must have found what he was looking for because he palmed something in his right hand, there in the shadows.

Ray sighed audibly. "You shouldn't go back there," he said, glancing at the kid under the momentary glare of the streetlights.

The kid was calculating numbers again, writing them in the air in front of his face. "One," he said. "One point four one four . . . one point seven three two . . . two . . . two point two three six . . ."

Ray pulled into a Safeway parking lot, empty in the early morning hours, illuminated only by a couple of streetlamps. He smiled at the kid. "You really like numbers, don't you?"

The kid looked at him with an expression Ray had never seen on his face before. It was the expression of a hawk looking at its prey. "Negative gravitational energy cancels the positive energy of matter," the kid said. His voice was gruff. "You're the one who stole my ukulele."

The kid bent forward toward Ray like he had something confidential to tell him. It was too late by the time Ray saw the open jackknife in the kid's right hand. He felt a jab in his belly as the kid leaned into him. It felt like nothing more than a good solid punch in the gut, but when Ray looked down and saw the inky blood seeping into his white shirt, he knew something was wrong. He looked up at the kid's face, but the kid refused to look at him. Unclasping his seatbelt, the kid popped the passenger's side door and let himself out of the car. He scurried away in the direction of the beach.

Sitting there in the Safeway parking lot, Ray thought he could hear the Pacific Ocean beating relentlessly against the shore of Kailua Beach. Or maybe it was his own breathing. And then he knew that this was what he had been waiting for all along.

He sat in the Nissan and felt the warm night air descending around him. Soon, it would be dawn. He sat in the Nissan and watched as the yellow lamps in the parking lot faded to a garish haze.

ACKNOWLEDGMENTS

Several stories in this collection were written and workshopped at the Wellstone Centre in the Redwoods and the Hambidge Centre in North Georgia. "Los Diablitos" was first published in the *Cold Mountain Review* and "Respite" first appeared in the journal *Intima*.

The author would like to thank his writing group comrades Dave Carpenter and Dave Margoshes. For several years now, I've had the great pleasure of writing and comparing notes with the two of them. Many thanks, as always, to my wife, Bev, and my sons, Wilson, Eric, and Connor.

ABOUT DWAYNE BRENNA

Dwayne Brenna is the award-winning author of several books of humour, poetry, and fiction. Coteau Books published his popular series of humorous vignettes entitled *Eddie Gustafson's Guide to Christmas* in 2000. His two books of poetry, *Stealing Home* and *Give My Love to Rose*, were published by Hagios Press in 2012 and 2015 respectively. *Stealing Home*, a poetic celebration of the game of baseball, was subsequently shortlisted for several Saskatchewan Book Awards, including the University of Regina Book of the Year Award. His first novel, *New Albion*, about a laudanum-addicted playwright struggling to survive in London's East End during the winter of 1850-51, was published by Coteau Books in autumn 2016. *New Albion* won the 2017 Muslims for Peace and Justice Fiction Award at the Saskatchewan Book Awards. It was also one of three English-language novels shortlisted for the prestigious MM Bennetts Award for historical fiction. His baseball novel *Long Way Home* was published by Pocol Press in 2022, and his theatre history text *Nights That Shook the Stage* (McFarland Books) came out in the spring of 2023. His short stories and poems have been published in an array of journals, including *Grain, Nine, Spitball, The Antigonish Review, Intima,* and *The Cold Mountain Review.*

ABOUT SHADOWPAW PRESS

Shadowpaw Press is a traditional publishing company, located in Regina, Saskatchewan, Canada and founded in 2018 by Edward Willett, an award-winning author of science fiction, fantasy, and non-fiction for readers of all ages. A member of Literary Press Group (Canada) and the Association of Canadian Publishers, Shadowpaw Press publishes an eclectic selection of books by both new and established authors, including adult fiction, young adult fiction, children's books, non-fiction, and anthologies, plus new editions of notable, previously published books in any genre under the Shadowpaw Press Reprise imprint.

Email: publisher@shadowpawpress.com.

 facebook.com/shadowpawpress

 x.com/shadowpawpress

 instagram.com/shadowpawpress

AVAILABLE OR COMING SOON

Literary Fiction

Hello by David Carpenter

Elephant in the Room by Betty Jane Hegerat

Thickwood by Gayle M. Smith

Let us be True by Erna Buffie

The Lavender Child by Harriet Richards

Waiting for the Piano Tuner to Die by Harriet Richards

Dollybird by Anne Lazurko

Small Reckonings by Karin Melberg Schwier

Poetry

First Light, Last Light by Glen Sorestad

The Door at the End of Everything by Lynda Monahan

The Glass Lodge: 20th Anniversary Edition by John Brady McDonald

Phases by Belinda Betker

Stay by Katherine Lawrence

Literary Nonfiction

Tales This Side of the Elysian Fields by Trevor W. Harrison

Cupboard Love: A Dictionary of Culinary Curiosities by Mark Morton

The Crow Who Tampered With Time by Lloyd Ratzlaff

Backwater Mystic Blues by Lloyd Ratzlaff

www.ingramcontent.com/pod-product-compliance
Lightning Source LLC
Chambersburg PA
CBHW032307310726
48973CB00008B/2548

9 781998 273294